A RARE GROOVE

They both stood up suddenly and found themselves only inches apart. Simone intended to step out of the way so he could go past her, but she couldn't move. Instead, she let her eyes wander over the beautiful naked slabs of his chest, then down over the ripples of his stomach. He sucked in his breath sharply, causing the abdominal muscles to harden and quiver.

"I'm going to kiss you," Maxwell stated in a husky voice.

Simone didn't know if he was asking permission or giving a warning, but she lifted her head and closed her eyes.

She first felt his hand cup the back of her head, then the soft brush of his lips against hers. His other hand settled at the base of her spine and pulled her up against the strength of his body. The kiss suddenly became open and wet with his tongue stroking and teasing hers. Simone moaned at the delicious sensations that were coursing through her body. Both her hands were spread wide on the planes of his back.

Also by Sophia Shaw

Shades and Shadows

Depths of Desire

Published by Kensington Publishing Corporation

A RARE GROOVE

SOPHIA SHAW

Kensington Publishing Corp.
http://www.kensingtonbooks.com

DAFINA BOOKS are published by

Kensington Publishing Corp.
850 Third Avenue
New York, NY 10022

All Kensington Titles, Imprints, and Distributed Lines are
available at special quantity discounts for bulk purchases
for sales promotions, premiums, fund-raising, and educa-
tional or institutional use. Special book excerpts or cus-
tomized printings can also be created to fit specific needs.
For details, write or phone the office of the Kensington
special sales manager: Kensington Publishing Corp., 850
Third Avenue, New York, NY 10022, attn: Special Sales
Department, Phone: 1-800-221-2647.

Dafina and the Dafina logo Reg. U.S. Pat. & TM Off.

ISBN-13: 978-0-7582-2029-5
ISBN-10: 0-7582-2029-4

First mass market printing: July 2008

10 9 8 7 6 5 4 3 2 1

Printed in the United States of America

To Naima Rebecca Shaw
Naima *(NAH-ee-mah)*

Content (Arabic), Graceful (Swahili)

ACKNOWLEDGMENTS

To my dad, Arnold Jackson, and my brother, Roland Jackson, for providing me with such great information and details about the beautiful Jamaican countryside and a little town called Goldmine.

To my agent, Sha-Shana Crichton—thank you for believing in me, and for your continued support and guidance.

To my editor, Rakia Clark—You make the process easy! I look forward to continuing to work with you.

Chapter 1

"You're listening to GROOVE FM 99.1," announced the silky, sultry voice over the radio. "Atlanta's home for classic soul. This is Moni S taking you on a musical joyride. It's 2:50 p.m. on your midday, and we've just ended fifteen minutes of music with Georgia's own Jean Carn singing 'Don't Let It Go to Your Head' from her second album, *Happy to Be With You*.

"Folks, I will be away next week, but Sweet Marie will be here to take care of you. It's Friday, so have a beautiful weekend. Right now I'm going to leave you with Eugene Record, 'Trying to Get to You,' on GROOVE FM 99.1."

The music faded in just as Simone turned off the microphone and swung her chair away from the computer screen.

"Good show, Moni," said her producer, Michael Thompson. "We got about thirty text messages during that last rare groove hour, not to mention a whole slew of e-mail."

Simone smiled. Her show, called the *Midday Joyride*, ran from 10:00 a.m. to 3:00 p.m. Monday to Friday. A large number of her audience listened in while at work, and were always letting her know how they felt about the music she played. GROOVE FM was very different from the other radio stations in Atlanta. It was a small family-run business with a very specific market: rhythm and blues, soul, and funk from the 1970s, 1980s, and early 1990s. It was the type of music that everyone loved.

Michael and Simone both started to clean up the studio and file away the session's reports. Don Appleby, the on-air host for the afternoon rush hour, took over the microphone and prepared to start his show after the commercial and news break.

"Are you all set for your vacation?" Michael asked Simone once they had left the studio and started walking out of the building.

"Just about," she replied.

"I can't believe you're going to Jamaica," he stated with a big grin on his face.

"I know," she agreed. "I can't wait to relax on the beach."

"What time is your flight on Sunday?"

"About eight thirty in the morning," Simone replied with a grimace. "It will put me in Jamaica before ten thirty. Amy's wedding isn't until Friday, but we're having a four-day bachelorette party."

Up until about one year ago, Amy Tomkin was the receptionist at GROOVE FM. She was a bubbly, friendly girl, so when she left the station, she remained close with many former coworkers, Simone in particular. Her fiancé's mother was Jamaican, so when they decided on a wedding in Jamaica, she asked Simone to be her maid of honor. Simone accepted with pleasure.

"That's pretty early," Michael commented in reference to her flight.

"I know! I'm going to have to be at the airport

before seven o'clock! I'm not looking forward to it. I am definitely not a morning person."

Michael laughed as he nodded with full agreement. Even though they both were in the office around nine o'clock in the morning, Simone could not crack a smile until at least eleven o'clock. She was a true professional, so the audience definitely could not tell the difference. But everyone in the studio knew to ignore her grumpy, sarcastic comments until her energy kicked in.

"How is Amy doing?" Michael asked.

"She's doing well. I thought she would be stressed out planning everything, but she said it was so easy. The hotel took care of everything."

"She and Cedric have been dating for as long as I've known her," he commented.

"I know. Almost ten years, she told me. They met in high school as freshmen. Isn't that romantic?" Simone said.

Michael just shook his head and twisted his lips, indicating he thought it was pretty sad. Simone continued, ignoring his cynical male perspective.

"And now they are getting married in paradise."

He couldn't help but smirk again. Simone was probably the most stunning woman he knew. Not only was she pretty, but she had this natural sex appeal that very few men could ignore. It wasn't just the sophisticated feminine clothes, or her perfectly manicured appearance; it was in her eyes, her smile, and even the way she walked. But anyone who knew Simone well knew that she was genuinely unaware of her sexual allure or the power it could have if used. She was a hopeless romantic that still believed in marriage and everlasting love.

A few minutes later, they were ready to part ways in the parking lot.

"Give Amy and Cedric my best."

"I will," Simone agreed before the two hugged. "See you in a week and a half."

"And don't go falling for an island man!"

She laughed out loud at his stern advice and was still smiling as they waved to each other from their cars on their way out of the parking lot.

The radio station was in the core of downtown Atlanta, so Simone headed toward the I-85, then north to Buckhead where she lived. Her apartment was in the heart of the booming suburb, near high-end shopping, trendy restaurants, and a vibrant nightlife. She was probably paying more than she should for a one-bedroom rental, but it was perfect for her needs right now.

When she got home, Simone turned on the stereo and headed into the bathroom. *The Best of Sade* played loudly while she filled the deep soaker tub with hot water and dropped in a moisturizing bath bomb. She then lit a series of lavender candles before removing her clothes and stepping into the water. The foamy bubbles covered her up to her neck.

Taking a long soak was Simone's favorite way to unwind after a show. However, on this afternoon, she would have to cut it short. She had a couple of appointments and several errands to do on Saturday, so her cleaning, laundry, and packing needed to be finished tonight. It had been at least a couple of years since she had gone away for more than a weekend, so Simone had no clue what she would need for a week in Jamaica that included a wedding and a prenuptial dinner.

She was also expecting a call from Kevin Johnson, the guy she was dating, later in the evening. He had left that morning for a business trip in Las

Vegas, so they would not see each other again until she returned from her trip. She wasn't sure if he would still call since their last talk had resulted in a heated argument the night before.

Kevin was a retired professional boxer, and now owned a successful car dealership in the Atlanta area. He was born and raised in Atlanta, and was a real live version of the rags-to-riches story. The public and media loved him, so he was often asked to attend or speak at social events. He had invited her to a charity dinner Thursday evening, but Simone had decided not to go at the last minute. As someone in the media herself, she understood his life, but it still made her uncomfortable to stand beside him in the spotlight. She liked being in the radio industry because she could maintain a certain amount of anonymity and privacy.

She and Kevin had been dating for only about eight weeks, seeing each other about once a week. The event on Thursday would have been the second large social event they would attend together. The first was on their second date, and Simone had felt as if she were under the microscope all night long. It was not an experience she wanted to repeat so soon.

Kevin was not pleased when she canceled at the last minute, and could not understand her aversion to hanging on his arm at an expensive, high-society affair. Even after Simone had apologized for the third or fourth time, but made it clear that she was not going with him to the dinner, Kevin had called her a few names and hung up the phone. They had not spoken since.

Simone eventually stepped out of the bathtub and wrapped herself in a plush white robe. She threw on comfortable cotton clothes and got busy with her list of chores. By ten thirty, she was finished packing, except for a few toiletries and clothes she intended to buy on Saturday.

She had left a message on Kevin's cell phone during her dinner break a couple of hours earlier, but he still had not called back. She was tempted to call him again, but resisted the urge. Her pride said that if he wanted to stay angry with her, she was not going to chase him down. Simone went to bed shortly after.

Saturday started early with a hair appointment at nine o'clock for a relaxer touch-up and cut. Simone had planned to be out of the salon by noon, but her stylist, Tony, had triple-booked himself with a last-minute wedding party. Tony was extremely apologetic and promised to have her done in record time. Though he used an assistant to speed things up, Simone still did not leave the salon until almost two o'clock. As irritated as she was by the delay, Simone had to admit that her hair looked fierce. Tony had outdone himself with the style, giving her a short, sculpted cut with an angled fringe at the front and tapered low along her nape. It lengthened her square face and showed off her high cheekbones and cat-shaped eyes. He also took the time to show her how to style it in the Caribbean heat so it would be low maintenance on her trip. She could not have been happier with the results.

But the delay still ruined her schedule for the day. In the end, after running around for the next several hours, Simone did not get home until almost eight thirty that night. She finished her packing and final preparations, then crawled into bed, exhausted, just before midnight. She was up again at a quarter to five the next morning feeling as if her head were stuffed with cotton. The day then went from bad to worse.

Her cab was over twenty minutes late, so Simone ended up in an extremely long line at the airline check-in counter. Then, after shuffling along for almost forty-five minutes, she stood in front of the reservation representative, but suddenly could not find her passport. She spent the next couple of minutes in a mad panic, riffling through her oversized purse as pens, gum, and miniature toiletries tumbled on the floor around her. Finally, she found it between the pages of a paperback novel, then had to pick up all her spilled items while the woman in line behind her tapped stiletto heels in annoyance.

Eventually, Simone made it to the boarding gate and even had a few minutes to grab a large coffee and a bagel. Her cell phone rang just as they were getting ready to board the plane. Simone debated whether or not to answer the call, then got concerned it might be urgent. She almost spilled the coffee trying to grab the call before it went to voice mail. It was Amy.

"Hey, Simone, I'm glad I got you," Amy said in a relieved voice. "I thought you may be on your flight already."

"We're just about to board. Is everything okay?"

"No," Amy replied after a long sigh. "We're not going to be flying out today."

"Why? What's wrong?" Simone asked urgently.

"Cedric has food poisoning or something. He's been throwing up since the middle of the night, and now he can't leave the bathroom. I think we're going to have to go to the hospital."

"Oh no! What did he eat?"

"I don't know! He was out with his work friends for

most of the evening. Anyway, our flight leaves in a few hours, but I'm trying to reach our travel agent."

"Oh, Amy!"

Simone was about to ask more questions, but she heard the final boarding call announced for her flight.

"Amy, I have to go. I'll call you once I land, okay?"

"Okay."

"I'm sure it's nothing serious," Simone added. "Tell Cedric that I hope he feels better soon."

"Okay," Amy answered. "Have a safe flight."

Simone hung up and rushed to the gate before they closed it off. Once she was seated, it took her a while to get comfortable and settled. Her thoughts were mixed with concern for Cedric, sympathy for Amy, and wondering what she was going to do by herself on a Caribbean resort until they arrived.

Soon after takeoff, Simone was served breakfast and a glass of champagne. Eventually, she relaxed and even managed to sleep for over an hour. She woke up when their pilot announced the descent to Sangster International Airport in Montego Bay, Jamaica. He added that the temperature at ten o'clock in the morning was a sunny seventy-seven degrees Fahrenheit. Simone lifted the window screen and got her first view of the island as they approached from the west off the Caribbean Sea. Frothy blue water met creamy beaches and lush green vegetation covering rolling hills.

She smiled at the sight and started feeling more excited than she had in weeks.

Three hours later, Simone walked into the third-floor hotel room she was supposed to share with Amy until after the wedding on Friday afternoon.

She had spent the last hour since she arrived on the resort property having refreshments and listening to a presentation about the facilities while the room was being prepared. She also tried to reach Amy, but could not get an answer at the home number or on her cell phone.

Their room was a spacious suite with two queen beds and a separate sitting area that had a sofa, desk, and television. There was also a small balcony that faced the garden.

Simone's luggage had been brought up while she checked in, and was lying neatly on a bench next to the closet. She dropped her purse on her suitcase, then kicked off her shoes before falling back onto the bed closest to the window, claiming it as her own. Part of her wanted to curl up under the covers and take a nap; the other part wanted to change into shorts and flip-flops and walk around the grounds. She debated the options for so long that she eventually fell asleep.

She did not notice the voice mail message on her cell phone until midafternoon. After the nap, she took a shower and was unpacking some of her clothes into the closet when she heard the phone beeping. The display indicated a missed call from Amy. Simone used the room phone to listen to her message.

"Hey, Simone, it's Amy. Cedric and I are back at home. He did have a mild case of food poisoning, but the doctors said he should be fine in a couple of days. I'll call you later and let you know when I've rescheduled our flights. Sorry to leave you stranded, but we'll get there as soon as we can. Speak to you soon. Bye."

Simone looked around the room wondering what to do.

After she finished getting settled, she stepped out onto their small balcony and into the warm, breezy Caribbean air. The June weather in Atlanta was about the same temperature, but somehow the warmth of the sun felt different here. She leaned her hip against the rail and looked around at the vibrant garden spread before her.

Simone was about to turn away from the view and head back into the air-conditioned room when a flash of color caught her eye.

That was the moment she saw him for the first time.

Chapter 2

Simone was surprised to see a small swimming pool to the right of her room, secluded behind a row of low bushes and towering palm trees. He emerged from the water as he finished his swim. His back was to her and he slowly walked through the water toward the pool edge. Each step he took caused sunlight to reflect off his dark wet skin. His shoulders were thick and broad, then bunched with power as he used his arms to push his body out of the pool and swing his legs onto the patio around it. The water ran down his back in tiny rivers, then soaked into the red material of his swim shorts. The trunks rode low on his slender hips and clung to the tight round curve of his butt. She caught a glimpse of powerful thighs and calves before they were hidden behind the plants and foliage.

From what she could see, this man was the physical embodiment of masculinity. He had to be over six feet, and was all smooth skin and lean muscles. The way he moved suggested easy confidence.

The stranger reached for a towel that lay on a nearby lounge chair, and leisurely rubbed the short black hair on his head. Simone continued to watch his every move as he wiped off his shoulders and each arm before wrapping the towel low around his hips and securing it in place by tucking in one of the edges. She even leaned a little closer, anticipating the moment he would turn around. Her silver earrings flashed in the daylight and must have caught his eye. He turned around quickly and looked straight up at her, one hand shielding his eyes from the bright sun.

Simone froze, unsure of how to react. Should she turn away and pretend she didn't see him, or wave at him and hope he waved back? They looked at each other so long that it was too late to do anything. She felt her face go warm with embarrassment, but she still could not look away. To her surprise and delight, Mr. Tall and Dark dropped his arm and spread his generous lips into a wide smile, revealing perfect white teeth.

She flashed a quick smile of her own, then hurried off the balcony with her heart racing. Once in the hotel suite, she burst out laughing, charged with energy from the encounter. A few minutes later, she stepped out onto the balcony again, but the pool area was empty and her beautiful mystery man was gone.

It was only a few minutes after three o'clock. Simone decided to go for a swim, and the secluded pool downstairs seemed like the perfect spot. She quickly changed into her new two-piece white bathing suit and added a matching white tunic over it. She coated her exposed skin with sunblock, then threw her sunglasses, towel, novel, and room pass into a beach bag and headed downstairs.

It took a little bit of investigating before she found the right path in the garden that led to the secluded pool. It was still empty when she finally found it. She dropped her bag on the tiles, then tried to pull one of the three lawn chairs a little closer to the pool edge with one hand. It was made from a thick iron and much heavier that she expected. Her first tug only moved it about an inch. She leaned forward and pulled again harder with both hands. The sunblock lotion had left her fingers a little greasy and caused her grip to slip. Simone stumbled backward, then tripped over her bag. She went tumbling into the water with her arms and legs flailing.

Simone was not a very good swimmer and panic set in immediately. It took her a few seconds to realize that someone was in the pool with her and was trying to help her. Solid arms wrapped around her chest and quickly lifted her up and out of the water. She coughed roughly and tried desperately to gulp in air.

When her heart rate had decreased and she had calmed down, Simone found herself lying on the same lounge chair that had caused the mishap to begin with. She closed her eyes and took a few more deep breaths.

"Are you okay?"

The deep voice caught her off guard. Simone turned quickly to her right and looked into eyes so black they shone. His long, angular face was marked with lines of concern. She blinked repeatedly, trying to find her voice. Then that familiar brilliant smile appeared on his face.

"Oh!" she uttered, immediately realizing it was the stranger from earlier.

"Are you okay?" he asked again.

The smile was still in place and he now seemed more amused than worried. His voice was as smooth and velvety as his skin.

Simone cleared her throat. Water gathered in her eyebrows from her soaking hair and dripped down her nose. She wiped it away with the palm of her hand.

"I . . . I think so," she managed to croak out after a few seconds. She turned her face away and tried to stifle another rough cough. When she looked back at him, the smile had faded and the look of concern was back.

"I don't know how to thank you," she whispered.

"Don't worry about it. I was just walking by when I heard you scream."

Simone then noticed that he was wearing a light blue T-shirt and khaki shorts instead of his red swim trunks. The clothes were dripping wet and plastered to his body.

"Are you sure you're okay?" His question forced her eyes away from his chest and back to his face. "Let me help you back to your room."

"Oh," she uttered as he gently took hold of her arm and helped her up. "I'm okay, really."

He ignored her protest, picked up her bag, and urged her forward with one arm across her back.

Simone gave in to his maneuvering and followed him toward her wing of the hotel. He didn't ask for directions until they were inside the building, and it then dawned on her that he recognized her from earlier. Her embarrassment doubled.

"My name is Maxwell, by the way. Maxwell Harper."

He had just let her go so that she could open her room door. The amused smile was back on his face.

"Nice to meet you, Maxwell Harper." She couldn't help but respond with a smile of her own. "I'm Simone St. Claire."

Maxwell nodded once.

When the door unlocked, Simone pushed it open and stepped over the threshold. She turned to face him while still in the doorway.

"Thank you, again. Thank God you were walking by when you did. And I'm sorry I got you all wet."

"No worries," he replied with a shoulder shrug.

"Okay, well . . . I guess I'll see you around the resort."

"How about for dinner?"

Simone just looked at him, not sure she had heard him correctly.

"I'm sorry," he quickly added and took a step back from the door. "You're here with your boyfriend or husband, right?"

She shook her head. "No. No, I'm not. I was supposed to meet my girlfriend, but she can't get here for another couple of days."

"Oh, okay." The smile was back. "So, would you like to meet for dinner?"

"All right," Simone replied before she could consider the wisdom of her decision.

"All right," he echoed. "How about I pick you up here at six o'clock?"

"Six o'clock it is."

Maxwell nodded again, then handed her the beach bag before he left.

Her conscience acted up while she was showering again to wash away the chlorine from the pool. She should not be going out with another man while she was technically dating someone else. Especially a man that made her feel warm in her stomach just by looking at him. But then she reasoned that she was on holiday, and it was a harmless dinner with another vacationer. Plus, it was now three days since she had heard from Kevin, and at this rate, their first fight might be their last.

Maxwell returned as scheduled, and Simone met him in the hall. After a brief greeting, they made their way toward the dining area of the resort in silence. Simone spent most of that time checking him out with her peripheral vision. As she had suspected, he had to be at least six feet three inches tall. She was a tall girl at five feet nine in her bare feet. Tonight, she was wearing sandals with a low heel, yet the top of her head just cleared his collarbone.

"How are you feeling?" he asked once they had been walking outside for a couple of minutes.

"I'm fine. My throat is a little sore, but that's it."

"Good."

"I just can't believe that I fell into the pool like that."

"You fell in? I thought you were trying to swim."

"No! I'm not the best swimmer but I'm not that bad," she told him. "I was just trying to move the chair closer to the pool, but my hand slipped. The next thing I know, I'm falling backward into the water."

Simone was laughing by the end of the story. He was laughing too, and it came out in a low, melodic hum.

Maxwell directed her toward one of the several restaurants that overlooked the ocean. He opened the door for her, then escorted her in with a light hand on her lower back.

"I think we might need reservations here, Maxwell," she told him while they waited to be greeted. "At least, I think that's what they said at the orientation this morning."

The hostess arrived before he could respond.

Maxwell gave his last name, and they were quickly seated in front of a window with a view of the beach.

"I had made reservations for myself yesterday when I arrived," he told her.

Simone nodded. Their waiter arrived and took their drink and meal orders.

"So, Maxwell Harper, what brings you to Jamaica?" she asked.

"Family," he said simply.

"Really? Like a reunion?"

"Sort of."

She nodded, a little perplexed by his short, cryptic answers.

"Are you all staying at the resort?" she asked, trying to understand him but not be too nosey.

"No, I think I'm the only one right now. Most of them are staying with my aunts and uncles in Mo Bay."

"So you're Jamaican? You sound American," stated Simone, unable to mask her surprise.

Maxwell smiled easily, dispelling her feeling that he was being evasive. "Both actually. Born in Jamaica, raised mostly in Atlanta."

"No way!" exclaimed Simone. "I'm from Atlanta. Which part?"

"College Park."

"I grew up around Druid Hills, but I live in Buckhead now. That is such a coincidence. Who would have thought I would come all the way to the Caribbean and the first person I meet is from the ATL!"

They spend the rest of their time at dinner in conversation about growing up in Georgia. Simone ended up doing most of the talking, sharing stories about high school and the neighborhood she grew up in. She was not normally so chatty, particularly with someone she had just met, but Maxwell made her feel as though he was really listening. Whenever she asked him a question, he answered briefly but then bounced a question back to her. By the time they finished dinner, Simone felt very self-conscious about how much she had shared and how little she had learned about him in exchange.

Once outside the restaurant, they started to walk back to her wing of the hotel. They were passing the main entrance to the resort and heard a calypso band playing not far away. They stopped and watched a growing number of people heading toward the music. Maxwell used his head to wordlessly suggest they find out what was going on. Simone nodded in agreement and they ended up on the beach in front of a makeshift stage and dance floor. A few people were already grooving to the music, but most were seated in the rows of chairs that had been brought outside and watching the performance. Cobalt blue water and the golden colors of the setting sun made the perfect backdrop.

Simone and Maxwell sat near the back.

"This is exactly what I pictured when I imagined this trip," Simone said in a soft, dreamy voice.

Maxwell glanced at her as though he saw something familiar on her face.

"Ahhh. This is your first time in the Caribbean, isn't it?" he asked.

"Yeah," she admitted, somewhat embarrassed. "My first time outside the United States, actually."

"I've come back many times, and I still get surprised at how beautiful it is," he told her. "So, what are you going to do with yourself until your friend arrives? Sit on the beach and get a tan?"

Simone heard the teasing in his voice and laughed in response. "I don't know. There's probably not a lot a girl can do by herself. I was going to check out the tours and excursions. Maybe go to see that waterfall that you can climb."

"Dunn's River Falls?"

"Yeah, that's it. And, yes, spend some time hanging out at the beach."

Maxwell now laughed at her teasing, and his darks eyes glittered. "So, do you want to see the Jamaica that the tourists see, or do you want me to show you the real Jamaica?"

Chapter 3

Simone stayed with Maxwell on the beach until well after midnight. They spent some of the time dancing and watching the performance. But mostly, they talked about his plans for the next couple of days.

Maxwell explained that he was born in a small town called Goldmine on the border of the Clarendon and St. Catherine parishes in the center of the island. He had not been back there since he was a young boy, and was heading there on Monday.

"I left Jamaica when I was about three years old, then came back every summer until I was eleven years old. I remember those trips so clearly. Like how black it was at night. There were no streetlights or anything, so if you were just a few feet from the house, you couldn't see anything that wasn't right in front of your face. But everyone walked around in the dark like it was nothing. They didn't even carry a lantern or anything."

"Wow, that sounds pretty scary," interjected Simone.

"You would think so, but I don't remember being scared," he explained. "There was one night when I was at my uncle's house after sunset for some reason. My older cousin had to walk me home, and she was only a couple of years older than me. I was about seven and she was nine years old at the most. She walked straight to my house through the woods without hesitation. I had to stay right on her heels so I didn't lose her. Then she dropped me off and walked back alone. I can't imagine it now, but I guess everyone just really knew the land."

He told her a few other stories about what he could remember of life in a small country town. Simone had grown up in the city all her life, so the details fascinated her.

She watched him speak, completely engrossed.

"It sounds beautiful," she told him.

"It was. I don't know what it's like now. The population was less than three hundred people in my mom's day, and I'm sure it's much less than that now. I even heard that there is some gold exploration in the area. So I'm sure a lot has changed. Last I heard, one of my uncles and several cousins still lived in the area."

"Do you have a big family?"

"Huge," he said with a laugh. "Between my mom and Pops, there must be about twenty aunts and uncles. God knows how many cousins."

"Are they all going to be at the reunion?"

Maxwell looked away from her to stare out at the ocean. He took so long to respond that Simone was about to ask him what was wrong.

"No. Just a few on my mom's side," he finally replied. "How about you? Do you have a large family?"

"Not really. I'm an only child, and so was my mom. My dad has a brother somewhere, but they were never close. But I always wanted a big family with a house full of noisy kids. Sounds silly, I know."

Simone forced herself to shut up. She had no idea why she was sharing such intimate information. He was going to think she was a freak.

"It's not silly at all," he told her simply.

She looked at him, but he was looking off into the distance again.

There was a comfortable silence between them for a while, and they listened to the music and watched the people dancing. One gentleman in particular had absolutely no rhythm, but he clearly didn't know it. He twisted and bounced enthusiastically to an odd beat that only he could hear. Simone and Maxwell stared at him for a while, then looked at each other before sharing a discreet laugh.

"How are you going to get to Gold Mine? Are you driving?" asked Simone after a while.

"I have hired a driver for the day. We're going to leave pretty early. Around nine o'clock."

Simone nodded, already calculating how early she would have to wake up in order to get ready, eat breakfast, and be on time. *If* she decided to go, of course.

She hadn't really taken his offer to see the real Jamaica too seriously at first. She assumed he was just teasing her. But the more he talked about his childhood, the more she considered the offer. The alternative was not much different than he had stated. What else was there for her to do by herself but sit on the beach or get pulled into a game of pool volleyball? From what she could see, the resort was beautiful and well appointed, but she would quickly get bored sitting around.

"So, do you want to come along?" Maxwell asked after a few seconds of silence.

"I . . ." she uttered, still uncertain how to respond, but he cut her off.

"I know you just met me, and you're probably wondering if I'm a sort of crazy killer hiding out in Jamaica. So before you answer, here is my card."

Simone watched him take out his wallet and remove a business card from its folds. Her mouth still hung open from her pause in speaking.

"And," he continued, "my room number is 9032. Now you can confirm my room with the hotel, and leave a note in your room pointing to me in case of your inexplicable disappearance. You can even Google me to see if I'm on the wanted list."

She took the card from him. He looked very serious, but Simone found herself laughing silently. Her shoulders shook with the effort to control her humor.

"What?" he demanded.

Simone shook her head, needing a minute to explain what tickled her. She giggled again.

"Nothing," she denied, shaking her head slightly.

"Okay, I know it's a little extreme but it's true. You don't know anything about me. It's better to be safe than sorry."

Simone was still grinning while she slipped his card into her purse.

"I wanted to say yes," she finally confessed. "But I was trying to figure out how to leave our information with the front desk so they would know where to look if I didn't come back. But your suggestion is much better."

She was laughing again by the end of the last sentence. Maxwell's face softened and he gave her a brilliant smile.

"All right, then. So now you have no reason to say no," he told her.

"I guess not."

By the time he walked her to her room, they had confirmed meeting for eight o'clock the next morning in front of the main restaurant. Once inside the suite, Simone immediately walked over to the phone to check for messages. She was relieved to see the red indicator flashing, and followed the instructions to retrieve the voice mail.

It was Amy.

"Hey, Simone, it's Amy. Good news. Cedric and I got a flight for Wednesday and we'll land there in the afternoon. He's feeling much better. I'm sorry you're there all by yourself, but it's probably worked out for the best. You can relax and get some rest. Maybe try some of the spa services they have. Anyway, I'll see you on Wednesday. Bye!"

Simone let out a long sigh, relieved to finally know what was happening in Atlanta. She kicked off her shoes before lying across the bed faceup.

Thank God things were going to be okay with Cedric, and the plans for the wedding. There was a moment earlier that day when Simone wondered if the whole thing would be called off. Amy would have been devastated. Instead, her voice sounded optimistic and excited again. Having her arrive on Wednesday still gave them two whole days to get ready for the ceremony. It wasn't the four-day party they had envisioned, but it was enough.

Simone thought back to Amy's suggestion that she get some rest and relaxation, and smiled to herself. If her friend knew how Simone had spent her evening and what she planned to do the next day, she would be shocked. So would all of Simone's friends. They constantly teased her about being the

stereotypical southern belle—pampered, manicured, and way too romantic.

Though Simone always denied it vehemently,
she knew deep down that some of it was true. She
was also secretly content with her traditional views
on how a woman should look and act. She had
learned them from her mother, the most beautiful
and feminine woman Simone knew. But, of course,
she could never let the girls know that. She was
supposed to be an ultraliberal professional woman
enjoying all the experiences Atlanta had to offer.

That was probably what made the planned trip
with Maxwell so exciting. It was totally out of character for her to leave a four-star spa resort to go off
into the hills of Jamaica and explore a tiny rural
village. She hadn't even brought the right shoes
for something like that! But there was no one
around to tell her it was a bad idea, or remind her
that she had just met Maxwell and knew next to
nothing about him. She didn't even know what he
did for a living!

Simone stretched like a cat on the bed and let
out another sigh. She remembered the business
card Maxwell had given her. It probably listed his
occupation, but she was too lazy to get up and get
it out of her purse. What did it matter anyway? She
wasn't looking for husband material; she already
had a boyfriend. Maxwell was just a competent
tour guide and travel companion. The fact that he
was sexy as hell was just a coincidence.

Eventually, Simone had enough energy to set
the alarm clock next to the bed. She then slipped
out of her clothes and under the covers before
falling asleep. Her dreams were filled with calypso
music and naked flesh gliding through brilliant
blue water.

The alarm went off less than six hours later as scheduled. Typical of her nature, Simone struggled to roll out of bed, but a quick shower brought her to life. She quickly dressed in denim blue capris with a sleeveless polo-collar shirt in a soft yellow. By the time she finished getting ready, it was five minutes to eight o'clock and she was feeling surprisingly alert and energetic. She tied up her white running shoes, probably completely inappropriate for the terrain, and headed to breakfast.

Maxwell was outside the entrance of the large buffet restaurant a few minutes earlier than they had planned. He was still surprised that he had invited Simone along today, and even more surprised that she had agreed. Ever since he decided to be here for this coming weekend, he had been dreading it. He loved his family, and was even looking forward to seeing them for the first time in over nine years, but it was still going to be hard. There were a lot of things still unresolved and unsaid.

So he had booked these extra days for himself to have a little relaxation and fun. This trip to Gold Mine was the only thing confirmed so far, and he had intended to keep the next few days open to see what came up. He hadn't planned on meeting a woman, at least not for a holiday fling.

But now as Maxell watched Simone St. Claire walking toward him, he remembered her effect on basic male instincts. There was no reason not to spend his free time in the company of a beautiful woman.

As he continued to watch her approach unobtrusively, at least three men could not resist turning their heads to watch her pass them. She had a beautiful face with sparkling eyes and a generous, pouty mouth. Her shapely, firm curves held the promise of sensual delight. What on earth was a woman like this doing alone on a vacation without her man? It was a question that he had asked himself several times since they had met.

Maxwell had been a few steps away from the pool when he had heard her scream. He jumped in the water to help her, not realizing she was the woman on the balcony. Once he saw she was going to be okay, his panic subsided and he was able to look at her more closely. She was coughing hard and frantically wiping water out of her eyes, yet still managed to look like a *King* magazine centerfold. Her wet swim clothes revealed a gloriously feminine shape that would fit perfectly in his large hands with a little to spare.

When they met for dinner, those curves were hidden behind a soft, pretty dress. On any other woman, it would have appeared demure, even conservative. On Simone, it only teased him to see and touch what was underneath. The light fabric bounced with her full breasts and swayed with her hips as she walked. She was a woman blessed with a body designed to give pleasure. If things worked out, he might get close enough to experience some of it.

Chapter 4

The trip to central Jamaica started just after nine o'clock as planned. Their driver, who introduced himself simply as Winston, was waiting for them at the entrance of the resort, and standing beside a fairly new Suzuki SUV. Maxwell got into the front passenger seat and Simone sat in the back behind him.

It had rained in the early morning, leaving the air fresh and clean. The sun now shone in a cloudless sky, and most of the water had already evaporated. Simone was happy that Winston kept the windows to the Suzuki rolled down, letting in the sounds and smells of Montego Bay. Pulsing reggae music played on the stereo, blocking her ability to hear the conversation between the men. She was quite content to watch the city scenes that they passed by.

Maxwell turned to talk to her once they had merged onto the highway.

"We're going to take the highway along the coast to Ocho Rios, then south from there. Winston thinks it should take about three hours."

Simone nodded and smiled in response. The men went back to their conversation, and she watched the countryside go by. Most of the drive went by smoothly, except for the occasional herd of cattle wandering across the road. They passed through two small cities, Falmouth and St. Ann's Bay, as well as several smaller towns. On the outside edge of Ocho Rios, Winston pulled over onto the shoulder and stopped next to a shack that sold fruit and other foods. He stepped out of the car and approached the vendor, an older woman sitting on a stool under the shade of large tree. They hugged like family.

"How are you doing? Do you want anything to eat?" asked Maxwell as he turned in his seat to face her.

"I'm good," she told him. "I could do with a drink."

"Come, let's go see what she has," he suggested.

Simone followed him to the stand and looked around while he asked about refreshment. She was surprised at the variety of produce displayed, some of which she didn't recognize. She was inspecting one small fruit with yellow skin when Maxwell returned to her with two bottled drinks in his hands.

"That's a June plum," he informed her with a head nod at the object of her curiosity. "Do you want to try it?"

"I don't know. . . ."

"It's really good," he coaxed, then laughed at her facial expression that clearly showed her skepticism. "Come, we'll get a few things."

She took her drink from him, then watched as he collected a variety of fruits, including a couple of small yellow mangoes and a dark green avocado. The merchant, whom Winston introduced as Ms. Edna, took Maxwell's payment and put the purchases in a large plastic bag. She smiled widely at them both. It was then that Simone realized that she was probably somewhere in her seventies, even though she displayed the vigor and vitality of someone much younger.

The three of them were on their way again in a few minutes. Simone relaxed while sipping slowly at the cold pop called ginger beer. The sharp aftertaste made her cough a couple of times, but quickly quenched her thirst.

When they were near the center of Ocho Rios, Winston exited the highway so they could drive through the city. Maxwell pointed out some of the local landmarks to Simone, including the famous Dunn's River Falls and beach. Simone was surprised at the number of cultural and historical sites he mentioned, and secretly wished they could stop and walk around. Instead, she tried to catch a glimpse of the museums and centuries-old churches. There were also plenty of flashy new hotels and resorts to cater to the tourists.

Soon they were back on the highway and heading south into the countryside.

"We gonna go tru Fern Gully now," Winston told them.

"Where?" asked Simone, not easily able to understand his thick accent.

"Fern Gully," Maxwell repeated. "It's a valley filled with ferns and other plants. You'll see."

As he finished speaking, the sun suddenly disappeared behind a dense cover of tall trees, and the area around them became quiet and dark. It took a couple of minutes for her eyes to adjust, but when they did, it was just as Maxwell described. They were engulfed by a dense forest of ferns that seemed to extend for rolling miles in every direction. The whole world was green until they emerged from the valley a few miles later. The bright daylight caught Simone off guard. She turned in her seat to watch the dark tear in the sunshine recede in the distance.

After about thirty miles, they turned off the main highway and onto a two-lane road. Their progress slowed substantially as they maneuvered around potholes, bicyclists, and minibuses overflowing with passengers. They passed through a series of small towns, all of which presented a picture of humble country living. Men and women sold their meat and produce at rough market centers. The children were either outside for the lunch break in their school uniforms, or working barefoot alongside their parents. They were poor, but looked happy and healthy.

Finally, they stopped in a place called Rock River and pulled up to the front of a house with a general store attached to it. Winston went inside.

"He's going to ask for directions," Maxwell explained. "Gold Mine is not on the road map, but there is a track that should take us there."

Winston was back about five minutes later, and told Maxwell what he had learned.

"Him say tun pan de bridge, and da road de pan the lef."

Maxwell nodded, like the directions made perfect sense to him. They were on their way again. When they found the road, it was more of a worndown dirt path leading into a forest, and with barely enough room to accommodate the Suzuki. Winston turned onto it without hesitation.

They had driven for about ten minutes when they passed trucks and other machinery several miles off to their left. There was a large, faded sign that declared the boundary of property belonging to a mining company. The site looked abandoned with no signs of people or movement. Three miles later, they drove past the first house that lay at the out-skirts of tiny Gold Mine. Winston continued until they reached an intersection that appeared to be the center of town. He stopped in front of a house with three older people sitting on the front stoop. The group looked at them with open curiosity.

Maxwell and Winston went to talk to them, while Simone stood by the car and looked around. There were six or seven houses along the main road, each with a sizable lot filled with fruit trees. She could see a few more houses along the connecting street. The buildings were made of cement and looked fifty to sixty years old. A few had newer brick addi-tions.

She turned back to the men as they talked. Maxwell finally walked back to her.

"Well, it turns out that my uncle moved away several years ago after my grand-aunt died," he told her with disappointment. "Neither he nor anyone from my mom's immediate family has been back since."

"Oh no, Maxwell. That's so unfortunate," she told him, and rested a gentle hand on his upper arm. "Do you know anyone else here?"

"Not really. These guys remember me as a young boy, though," he replied with a nod toward the men still talking to Winston. "The community was probably only about four or five families to begin with, and now there are just two, along with a few men here to work the land. Most of the young people have been gone for years."

They both looked around for a few minutes, taking in the quiet beauty around them.

"What do you want to do?" she finally asked.

"Well, my grandparents' house is up the hill, and

there are fields of banana and orange trees behind it. One of my distant cousins has been staying there and taking care of the crop, they said. But he's gone to Spanish Town for a few days. We might as well go have a look around.

"Winston has some family nearby, in May Pen, that he is going to visit. I told him to come back for us in a couple of hours."

"Okay," she agreed.

The house was off the secondary road on top of a hill that overlooked the town. Winston dropped Maxwell and Simone off in front of the property, and they walked the rest of the way through a rough stone path. The front yard was overgrown with years of untrimmed grass, weeds, and other ground cover. The house was a low bungalow with a wooden front porch that wrapped around the exterior. It looked strong and well built but showed signs of neglect.

Simone followed Maxwell around to the back. They both stopped to look at the breathtaking view of the yard and the valley beyond. Near the house were several rough gardens bursting with different vegetables, and trees heavy with fruits. Behind that were rows and rows of orange trees leading down a shallow hill. Farther down was a basin filled with banana trees, then miles and miles of lush vegetation and rolling hills.

"Wow, Maxwell. This is unbelievable! Is all of this your grandparents' land?" she asked, still amazed at the natural richness around them.

"Yeah," he said simply. "Come, let's go for a walk."

They left Simone's purse and their bag of fruit on the porch and headed toward the fields. As they passed the gardens, Maxwell pointed out the different plants, including herbs, peppers, and peas, and a leafy vegetable called callaloo. Among the trees, he pointed to a curious red fruit called ackee.

"It's used in Jamaica's national dish, ackee and saltfish. But it's poisonous."

Simone stepped back in alarm. "What? And you guys eat it?"

He nodded, then picked up a ripe one off the ground and showed her the yellow flesh inside. "You have to wait until it's completely ripe and the blossom has opened before it's edible."

She looked at him, then back at the exotic fruit.

"And who tested it the first time to find that out?" she asked dryly.

It took Maxwell a couple of seconds to see her point; then he burst out laughing.

"I'm just saying, was it trial and error, or what?" she continued.

He laughed harder, which made her start chuckling.

When they both calmed down, he took her hand and they continued into the vast field of orange trees.

"Were these always here?" Simone asked.

"I think so," he replied. "I remember that my grandfather and my uncles would take the crops to the market a few times a year, but otherwise they would just trade the fruit locally for meat, or rice and cornmeal. For years, my mom would send them barrels of other goods, like flour, oil, or soap."

"Really? Why didn't she just send money? Wouldn't it be easier?"

"Not really. Those things are so expensive to buy here, especially when the Jamaican dollar is doing really badly. Plus, there is always the fear that people would steal the money, I think. And she used to include things that you couldn't get very easy here, like special creams and books that my grandmother liked."

Simone nodded, completely fascinated by the way of life that he was explaining to her.

"The area is so rich in land, and the weather is so perfect. It really is paradise. Why do so many people leave the island?" she asked.

"I guess it's like anywhere else in the world. The young people don't want to stay and be farmers or cultivators, and their parents want them to get educated, make money, and live a better life. And they thought that England or North America would offer them that opportunity. Now I think the children of those immigrants are seeing that financial wealth is not what it was cracked up to be. There is also land wealth and the freedom of not being tied to money and a paycheck. I know quite a few people who were born in America and have moved back to Jamaica, or plan to."

"What about you? Would you ever move back? Technically, this land is part yours, isn't it?"

"I don't know. Maybe someday. Even though I've lived in cities most of my life, I'll always be a country man," he told her.

They stopped under one of the trees, and Maxwell picked a large orange and quickly peeled off the firm skin with his fingers. He handed her the juicy fruit, then peeled one for himself.

Simone watched his strong, sure hands. "I could see you here."

Maxwell looked at her and their eyes connected. She looked away, a little embarrassed by his assessing stare. She had meant the remark to sound off the cuff, but instead, it came out as a compliment.

The more time they spent together, the more she

was fascinated by him. She had never met a man like him before. He was clearly confident, knowledgeable, and capable of taking charge, but never arrogant or condescending. Even when he told her about all the food that was new to her, she didn't feel ignorant or embarrassed. Instead, he made her feel safe, like he would take care of her in this foreign wilderness. No other man had ever made her feel that way.

The guys she knew in Atlanta liked to think they were in charge and knew everything, but the only thing they cared about was their cars, clothes, and newest gadgets. None of them would ever get their hands dirty to feed themselves.

Maxwell and Simone were both on their second orange when the breeze suddenly picked up and the sky darkened. They were halfway down the hill and about half a mile from the house. The leaves around them rustled loudly, and a flock of birds quickly flew away in protest. The first fat drop of rain came seconds later, and they were still under the orange tree when the sky opened up with a heavy downpour.

Chapter 5

"Damn!" exclaimed Maxwell under his breath.

He quickly grabbed Simone by the waist and pulled her farther under the tree. His back was up against the trunk and she was flush against him with her cheek against the top of his chest. Maxwell tried to cover her head with one of his arms. But it was useless. They were both soaked within a matter of minutes.

"Are you all right?" he shouted so she could hear him over the loud shower.

She nodded.

The storm had rolled in so fast that it caught him completely off guard. He then saw a flash of lightning far off in the distance. It became clear that they could not stay under the tree much longer, and the storm was going to last for a while.

"We're going to have to run to the house, okay?" he told Simone. "Are you ready?"

She nodded again.

Maxwell took her hand and they dashed together through the orchard. The loud boom of thunder caused Simone to startle, then stumble over an exposed root. She would have fallen if Maxwell had not quickly pulled her up again and into his arms. He gave her a few seconds of rest, and then they were off again. Once they were beyond the trees, the rain was so heavy that they could barely see in front of them. But Maxwell kept going, instinctively knowing exactly where the house was. Finally, they reached the covered porch.

They stood there for several minutes soaked to the bone and breathing heavily. It was still very hot and muggy, but Simone soon started to shiver in her wet clothes. The material was plastered to her.

Maxwell cursed again and pulled off his wet shirt. He used both hands to squeeze out as much water as possible.

"Take off your top," he told her gently.

At first, she looked at him with wide eyes, clearly surprised by his request. He suddenly felt like pulling her into his arms and warming her with his body.

"Take my shirt. You need to get out of your wet clothes," he explained, and held up his shirt so she could have some privacy.

"Thank you," she said, after doing as he suggested.

Maxwell took her top out of her hand and wrung it out also. At one point, he thought he caught her looking at his naked chest, but she turned away quickly. He could not help smiling to himself.

Another bolt of lightning struck, this time much closer to the house. The thunder rolled in right after.

"How long do you think this will last?" she asked.

"It's kind of hard to say. It could pass quickly, but to be honest, it looks like it will be here for a while."

Maxwell didn't want to tell her the worst of it. If the rain continued to come down this hard, there was a real possibility that the road back to Rock River could get washed out. He remembered that it was a common occurrence when he was a kid. They could be stuck in Gold Mine until the water level went down.

"Let's see if there is a way into the house," he suggested.

The front and back doors were locked, so they started opening the shutters to see if any of the glass windows were open. Finally, they discovered one at the side of the house that was unlatched. Maxwell pulled it open wide enough, then climbed in, and found himself in a small bedroom. It was very dark inside, but with enough light from the window to see into the main hall of the house.

He switched on a few lights, then let Simone in through the back door. She had their belongings in her hands. The air inside was very hot, but she still shivered. Silently, he took her hand and led her around until they found a simple bathroom. A quick search revealed several bath towels.

"Okay, why don't you get out of those clothes, and I'll try to find something dry for you to wear," he told her.

She nodded and tried to smile, but Maxwell could tell she was miserable. He took one of the towels with him, then closed the door to give her privacy.

He felt really bad about putting her in this situation. This wasn't exactly what he intended when he had invited her out for the day. Instead of showing her a good time on a posh resort like he should have, they were stuck eating whatever he could find in the cupboards of the house.

Maxwell cursed again and went to look for some clothes.

It was just bad luck that the rain came when it did. He had found Simone sexy as hell from the beginning, and was really enjoying hanging out with her.

She was easygoing and surprisingly funny. His male instincts told him that she found him attractive too and it was only a matter of time before they would act on the sparks between them. Maxwell was already thinking of how they could spend the next few days together. But it seemed unlikely now.

The master bedroom was at the back of the house. Maxwell stripped out of his wet shorts and briefs, then dried off with the towel. He found a brand-new pair of men's cotton pajamas still in the package. They were a size too small, but they would do until his clothes dried. He pulled on the pants, then left the shirt on the handle of the bathroom door for Simone to use when she was done.

In the kitchen, the cupboards were better stocked than Maxwell had anticipated. By the time Simone found him about fifteen minutes later, he had a pot of rice almost cooked, and a pan simmering with cabbage and salted fish. Hot water was boiling in the kettle.

Maxwell turned around when he heard her enter the room. She stood a couple of steps away from him in the pajama top. Because of her height, the edge only reached the top of her thighs. His eyes immediately went to the long length of her curvy legs. They looked firm and silky smooth. He watched her body move under the fabric as she walked past him over to the stove. When she bent over slightly to look in the pot, Maxwell could almost see the sweet curves of her buttocks. His body hardened immediately.

"Wow, this smells great, Maxwell," she exclaimed with her back still to him. "Where did you find this food?"

She sounded in good spirits, not at all upset about their unusual situation.

"There were a few things in the cupboard." His

voice came out deep and throaty, but Simone didn't appear to notice.

Suddenly, there was eerie silence around them. Maxwell and Simone looked at each other until they realized that the rain had stopped as quickly as it started. They went to the nearest window in time to watch the dark clouds receding. Simone turned to Maxwell with a bright smile, and he grinned back.

"It think it's over," she said excitedly. "That wasn't so bad."

"Where are your clothes?" asked Maxwell. "We can put them outside. They might be dry by the time Winston returns."

"They're in the bathroom," she replied. "Did you see any tea bags? I can make us some tea in the meantime."

Maxwell handed her a box he had found in the cupboard.

By the time he went outside with their things, the sun was shining again. There was a laundry line in the backyard. He took his time squeezing out excess water before draping each item over the wire and securing them with the wooden clothespins. Simone's bra and panties were the last in his hands. Maxwell handled the delicate black lace gently. It was exactly the type of lingerie he imagined she would wear: beautiful and obviously expensive. He could only imagine how she would look wearing them for him.

When he was finished, Maxwell breathed out and looked out over the vast land before him. He had to get control of himself. He had known the woman for only twenty-four hours and she was completely under his skin. How was that possible? Why was his mind constantly filled with visions of her in various states of nakedness? In a few days, they would go their separate ways and probably never see each other again. There was no point in getting attached.

He breathed out again and went back inside. Simone was sitting at the small table next to the kitchen and had set out two plates of food for them. She was sipping her tea, clearly waiting for him. He sat in the seat beside her.

"I can't believe how quickly the storm passed," she said to him. "It's almost as though we imagined the whole thing. Well, except for the part where we broke into the house and are eating someone's food and wearing their clothes."

Maxwell laughed heartily. "I'm sure my cousin won't mind. I'll leave him a note with some compensation."

"Thank you for taking me along today. And thank you for this delicious food," Simone told him after they had started eating.

"Are you serious? Some trip. We almost got stranded in the middle of nowhere in a thunder storm. Thank God the house was open," he replied.

"Well, it's turned out fine in the end. I've seen and learned so much. It's an adventure I'll always remember."

"Then it was my pleasure."

They continued eating in silence for a couple of minutes.

"So, what do you do back in Atlanta?" Simone finally asked him.

"I don't live in Atlanta anymore," Maxwell told her, noting the surprise on her face. When they had talked last night, he knew he had left her with the impression he was still living there. At the time, it seemed harmless. The conversation after hadn't warranted further explanation. Now, knowing she lived there made him miss the ATL for the first time in years.

"I moved to Toronto a few years back," he clarified.

"Really? Toronto, Canada? How did you end up there?"

"Well, my mom and I emigrated there when I was a baby and lived there until I was around six years old. We got our citizenship, but moved to Atlanta soon after."

"Really? So you're Jamaican, Canadian, and American?" she quizzed. "That's so weird."

Maxwell shrugged. "It's was pretty common as immigrants moved around to wherever they could find enough work to support their families."

"So, what do you do in Toronto?"

"I'm a civil engineer. The firm I'm with mostly does infrastructure and transportation work for the cities in the area."

"You mean like bridges and stuff?" she asked.

"Basically."

"Do you enjoy it?" she asked.

The question caught him off guard and he wasn't sure how to respond. Engineering was not a career he had chosen for himself. It had been forced on him by his pop, who was also an engineer. As a young man deciding what to do in college, Maxwell had wanted to study business and maybe start his own company, but it was out the question. There was no way Pop was going to help pay for him to study anything other than a true profession. Maxwell did as he was told, but with deep resentment. It wasn't until years later that he could admit to himself that he found his job really satisfying.

"I do," he told Simone.

"Why do you say it like that? Like you're surprised that you enjoy it?" she asked, looking at him quizzically.

Maxwell shrugged. "Ten or fifteen years ago, when I imagined my life, it wasn't what I pictured myself being, I guess. My pop is an engineer too, so I did it to please my family. But, somewhere along the line, I realized that I can't see myself doing anything else."

When he finished speaking, he looked up at Simone. She was leaning forward in her chair and had her head propped up by the fist of a bent arm. Her eyes never left his face. Maxwell could tell that she heard everything he said, but also understood the issues he didn't say. He wasn't sure if he had ever felt that level of nonverbal communication before. It made him a little uncomfortable.

"So, what about you, Simone? What do you do in Atlanta?"

"I do a radio show, actually."

"Oh yeah?" he said with surprise. It was his turn to lean forward, arms folded and resting on the table.

"Yup. It's the midday show on GROOVE FM. Have you heard of it? We play old school R and B, soul, funk, that sort of thing."

"Sounds familiar, but I haven't been back to Atlanta in years."

"Well, you can listen to it on the Web," she told him.

"Wow. So you're a celebrity!"

"Hardly," Simone denied with a shy laugh.

"How did you get into radio? Did you take it in school?" he asked, completely fascinated.

"I got my degree in journalism and hoped I would become a local news reporter, or something like that. But I made money in college by DJing at club parties."

"You're kidding!"

"I'm serious. Then I started playing soul and rare groove at after-hours parties."

"Rare groove?" he asked, not sure what she meant.

"Rare hits from the late seventies up to about the mid-nineties by major urban artists. Like the free songs that were on the B side of hit records. The title song on the A side would have been a chart topper, probably very commercial, very pop, but the B-side song was often much better. That's where the real soul sound and funk beats came from. So now there is an appreciation of those records. You see it all over the place, especially in hip-hop. They sample and remix those rare groove tracks all the time."

Maxwell listened quietly, captivated by her passion and knowledge about music.

"Anyway," she continued, going back to how she got into radio, "I was playing rare groove at these parties and that's where I met the music director at GROOVE. He offered me a job doing the midnight show. I got the midday show about three years ago."

Maxwell just shook his head, clearly speechless.

"I know. I don't look like the typical club DJ. You should have seen people's faces when I would show up with all my vinyl. I even went through a phase of trying to dress hip and funky, but I could never pull it off."

She laughed at the memory, and Maxwell smiled in response.

"I'm sure you looked beautiful regardless," he told her.

At first, Simone looked down at the table and her grin faded to a humble smile. But his words hung in the air between them, changing the mood from light conversation to something much deeper. When she raised her eyes again, he knew he saw a spark of heat and the reflection of what his eyes were saying. They remained frozen in that tableau for long seconds, neither of them willing to break the connection.

"Do you still want to be a reporter?" Maxwell asked after a while.

"I don't know. My friend Natasha works for a big newspaper, and the stories she tells me have kind of turned me off. She's trying to get her big break and eventually write real stories, but it's so political and competitive. But I think she will make it. She's one of those aggressive people that will not give up, no matter what. If she senses a story, she's like a dog with a bone. I'm not like that."

"Are you sure?" he asked.

Simone looked at him questioningly.

"I mean, you've managed to break into a very male-dominated world. That must take an impressive amount of guts and determination, I would think."

She became flushed with pleasure and looked down at the table. The only other person that had ever made her feel that empowered was her father. She didn't know how to respond to Maxwell. When their eyes met again, the sparks were tangible in the air.

"Maybe I should see if our clothes are dry," Maxwell finally said.

Chapter 6

They both stood up suddenly and found themselves only inches apart. Simone intended to step out of the way so he could go past her, but she couldn't move. Instead, she let her eyes wander over the beautiful naked slabs of his chest, then down over the ripples of his stomach. He sucked in his breath sharply, causing the abdominal muscles to harden and quiver.

"I'm going to kiss you," Maxwell stated in a husky voice.

Simone didn't know if he was asking permission or giving a warning, but she lifted her head and closed her eyes.

She first felt his hand cup the back of her head, then the soft brush of his lips against hers. His other hand settled at the base of her spine and pulled her up against the strength of his body. The kiss suddenly became open and wet with his tongue stroking and teasing hers. Simone moaned at the delicious sensations that were coursing through her body. Both her hands were spread wide on the planes of his back.

Maxwell pulled his head back and looked into

her eyes. His nose flared lightly as his breath came out in deep rushes. He laid a series of gentle pecks along her brow, as though trying to slow the passion between them. But his gentleness made her want to burn hotter. Simone slid her hands lower until they rested on the edge of his pants just above the solid roundness of his bottom. His mouth fell on hers again, now hot and urgent.

"Simone, you're driving me crazy," he uttered with his forehead resting on hers. "I want to look at you."

He let her go and leaned back, allowing enough room for him to undo each of the buttons of the pajama shirt. She could only watch, anticipating his eyes on her nakedness. When the top was undone, he brushed the sides away, revealing her full, firm breasts. Their chocolatey tips were hardened with excitement. He took a step back and looked down at all of her. She flushed under his intense inspection.

"You're the most beautiful thing I've ever seen."

Maxwell said the words with such assertion that Simone believed him. She felt completely sexy and powerful, and more aroused than ever before in her life. She wanted this man with a hunger and urgency that was indescribable and undeniable. She stepped to him, deliberately allowing her nipples to brush against his chest and silently begging him to touch her.

He groaned and kissed her again hard, then covered her tempting breasts with his big hands. His palms brushed repeatedly over her puckered flesh. Simone felt weak from the electricity that charged straight down the pit of her stomach. Molten wetness pooled at her core.

Maxwell moved his lips down her neck, then along her collarbone. He scooped her voluptuous curves in his hands, and gently licked the tips, first one, then the other. Then he sucked one deep into his mouth.

"Oh God!" she groaned as her knees went weak.

She groaned again when he did the same to the other nipple. He continued to play with her until Simone felt like she would faint from the assault.

"Turn around," he told her.

It took a moment for her to respond, surprised at the request and excited to find out what he had in store for her. Maxwell started near her ankle and slowly worked his hands, lips, and tongue up her legs. Simone closed her eyes tight and let her head fall back. Every inch of her body tingled in response.

"Amazing legs," she heard him utter between the soft kisses.

He stopped when he reached the very top of her thighs. She felt him stand up again, then felt the shirt slip off her body. There was silence for a few seconds. When she looked over her shoulder, he was looking over her body as though committing it to memory. When their eyes met, she sucked in her breath, surprised at the raw passion in his.

He held her gaze and brushed his palms up over the plump curves of her bottom. He squeezed and kneaded at the round flesh, clearly enjoying the shape and feel of them. Then he slipped both thumbs so low they almost brushed the core of her heat. Simone leaned forward, silently begging for the touch.

Maxwell's breath came out in a long, low moan. He brushed his thumbs deep again. She leaned forward a little more.

"Oh, Simone. You're killing me!"

He wrapped his arms around her rib cage and

pulled her hard against him. His hot erection was like a brand against her buttocks. His hand ran over her body with urgent strokes from her quivering breasts to her flat lower stomach.

The loud honk of a horn finally penetrated through their mingled whimpers of desire. They both froze.

"Damn!" Maxwell muttered. "It's Winston."

His hand remained on her breast for a few more seconds. He let out a deep sigh, then let go of her. Simone came crashing back to earth with cruel speed. She immediately felt chilled without the heat of his body against her. Maxwell handed her the cotton top and she slipped it on gratefully.

"Wait here. I'll go get our clothes."

Simone watched him walk away. He paused for a moment at the door, then went outside.

She looked around at the strange house they had broken into, a little shocked that she had been naked and panting just a few minutes ago. What had gotten into her?

Maxwell was back before she was able to do more than stack their plates together. He handed over her clothes, now dry and folded. Her bra and panties were on the top and she covered them with her hand, embarrassed that he had them in his hands. It was a ridiculous feeling considering what had happened between them.

Simone went into the bathroom to get dressed, and give him some privacy also. Once she had her own clothes on, she stood in front of the sink and looked in the mirror. Her face was bare of any makeup and shiny in the heat. Her hair was a mess, all frizzy and limp from being wet and drying naturally. She wet it again and used her fingers to tame it into a reasonable style. Once she felt ready, she went back into the hall of the house.

Maxwell was in the kitchen cleaning up the dishes and pots from their late lunch. She silently joined him to help.

"All set?" he asked once the kitchen was back in the shape they had found it.

"I think so," replied Simone.

She watched as he wrote a note with a pencil and paper he found near the fridge. He then counted out one hundred U.S. dollars and put it under the message. They left the way they came in.

Winston was standing outside the Suzuki patiently waiting for them. Maxwell joined him in the front and Simone sat in the back as before.

It was almost four o'clock when they left Gold Mine, and the drive back to Montego Bay had more traffic on the streets and highways. Many Jamaicans were on their way home from work or out visiting friends and relatives. They arrived at the resort just before seven thirty.

"Are you hungry?" Maxwell asked her as they walked through the front lobby.

"I am, but I really want to take a shower first," she told him.

"Good idea. Would you like me to meet you at your room at around eight thirty?"

"That sounds good."

They walked the rest of the way in silence.

Once inside her suite, Simone headed straight to the bathroom and peeled off her grungy clothes. The spray of the shower felt amazing, so she lingered for several minutes longer than usual. In front of the counter, she took her time lathering her body with rich scented lotion, then dried and styled her hair. She added a light sweep of makeup to her face, wanting to look fresh and natural in the Caribbean heat.

She was about to get dressed when she noticed a message on her cell phone. Simone had not taken it with her to Gold Mine, and the display noted that the call had come in earlier that morning.

"Simone, it's Kevin. Call me when you get this. I'm back in Atlanta."

That was it.

Simone hung up the phone and threw it on the bed with disgust. His voice had been short and emotionless. She could only assume that he was still annoyed with her. Not that he was usually warm and personable, she thought to herself.

In the eight weeks since they met, Kevin had been traveling almost every week. Their dates were mostly for dinner, including the benefit gala, and to the club twice. They talked on the phone maybe every other day, but only for a few minutes. Not once in that time did they have a personal conversation that lasted more than fifteen minutes.

Simone hadn't really thought about it until the drive back to the resort that evening. Kevin was a busy guy, always on his cell phone, or talking to groups of people. It was understandable as he managed personal appearances and his car dealership. She had tried to respect that. He was the most eligible bachelor in Atlanta, so it seemed silly for her to complain about it. Simone just assumed that they would continue dating and eventually find time for intimate conversation.

Yet, weeks later, she still felt no connection with him, physical or otherwise. They had kissed a lot, and even shared more intimate touches, but nothing more. He had asked her to stay over at his place after their last two evenings together, but she had declined. Their contact had been nice, but that was it. Nothing even close to the fireworks Maxwell Harper set off just by looking at her.

Simone sat at the edge of her bed and nibbled on her bottom lip.

Was this thing with Maxwell just a result of being on vacation in the Caribbean? She knew nothing about him beyond what they had discussed, and how would she know if any of it was true? Maybe it was the freedom of being away from the hustle of the city and the scrutiny of her friends that released her inhibition. Or the fact that he was essentially a stranger that she would never see again once their time together was over.

For all those reasons, Simone decided to indulge in whatever would happen between her and Maxwell. He was able to evoke a rare passion in her and at least she could go back to her regular life with the memories. A decision about Kevin could be made another day.

She finished getting dressed by slipping into a white cotton dress with a halter top and a wide-pleated skirt. The bodice tied around her neck, leaving the back bare. The deep V of the neckline lifted her breasts and presented an enticing cleavage. In the bathroom, Simone added a spritz of perfume to the base of her throat and a light coat of lip gloss. She added silver ballerina slippers on her feet, then went downstairs.

Maxwell was walking along the path to meet her when she stepped outside.

"You look great," he said in a smooth voice when he stopped in front of her.

The air between them was suddenly charged with sexual tension.

"Thank you," Simone replied graciously. "A lot better than I did this afternoon, I bet."

She laughed a little, hoping to lighten the mood. "You could never look as beautiful as you did this afternoon."

His eyes held hers, making it obvious exactly which image of her he held in his mind. Simone couldn't think of anything suitable to say. She let him take her hand and they walked to the large dining room for a buffet dinner.

Maxwell spent most of the time while they ate asking her about her radio show and how she became a DJ. She told him about her father's prize collection of records from early jazz to eighties hip-hop. Music was his only real hobby, and he was thrilled that Simone developed an appreciation for it also. He was not so happy about her DJing around the city, and often went with her to make sure she was safe. It definitely didn't help her look cooler at the club, she told him.

"What about your mother?" he asked at one point.

They were finished with their meal and were lingering at the table drinking white wine.

"Well, my dad and I didn't tell my mom," Simone told him with a sly grin. "We figured it was better not to stress her out. I resemble my mother in most ways, so I think my dad liked the fact that I took something from him. If she knew about it, my mom would definitely have made me stop, and my dad always supported what my mom wanted."

"It sounds like you are all very close."

"We are. I couldn't wish for better parents," she said.

Simone talked some more about her childhood, and Maxwell listened intently, occasionally asking questions. She asked him about a few things, but his answers were always brief and lacking in detail. There were clearly some issues with his family, but

Simone sensed they were too sensitive for him to talk about, so she respected that and didn't press.

"You're tired," Maxwell stated after she let out a series of delicate yawns. "Come, let me walk you to your room."

He helped her out of her chair and took her hand again, interlocking their fingers as they walked. It was a simple thing done unconsciously, but Simone loved the feel of the innocent touch. They stopped in front of her door and Maxwell turned her to face him. He took her face in his hands, using his thumb to brush the hair at her temples. They looked at each other for several moments, their gaze touching on each other's eyes, lips, nose, and brows.

"I don't know what this is," he told her finally.

His voice was just a little above a whisper.

"I've known you, Simone St. Claire, for one day, and I can't stop thinking about you." He pressed his lips on hers for a second. "I want to touch you, taste you, be inside you. I want to sleep naked with you and talk for hours."

Simone could only stare at him with her eyes wide and lips open, wanting to feel his mouth on hers again.

"I want too much too soon," he told her while releasing a long breath. "But we live in two different countries and in a couple of days we will move on with our lives. So I think I should leave you now."

It took Simone about a minute to understand what he was saying and to overcome the intense disappointment she felt. He wasn't going to come into her room and make love to her like she craved.

He kissed her again, hard and urgent, then stepped back. Simone fumbled with the pass key, but finally opened her door. She was about to say good night when Maxwell grabbed her wrist. She swung back to him, her heart racing with anticipation.

"Will you meet me for breakfast? At eight o'clock?"

She could only nod before putting the door between them.

Chapter 7

Maxwell was up before six the next morning, but spent almost an hour tossing under the sheets trying to catch a few more minutes of sleep.

After leaving Simone, he had changed into his swim shorts and gone back to the secluded pool in the garden, the place where he had met her. He dove in and swam lap after lap until he was exhausted. The intention was to work off the tension in his body and make him too tired to want her or think about her. It didn't work. He had burned the image of her incredible body into this mind, and it was there every time he closed his eyes.

His sleep, when it did come, was restless and uncomfortable and he woke up just as horny and irritated.

He was an idiot, Maxwell told himself while standing in a shower as cold as he could stand. He should have taken her to bed last night and done everything his body was craving for. He would have a smile on his face right now, rather than a painful case of frustration. It should be simple sexual release, but he had to go and make it complicated.

The reality was that, at thirty-one years old,

Maxwell was well past the stage of his life where he could enjoy meaningless sex with any willing woman. There had been enough of that in his teens and twenties, and it held no interest for him now. He was ready to meet a nice lady who could be his partner in life. He wanted to get married, have children, and plan for the future.

Back in Toronto, there were plenty of beautiful single women. Maxwell wasn't actively dating anyone now, but he had no doubt he would meet that special person in due time.

The last thing he needed was an irrational and uncontrollable attachment to a woman hundreds of miles away. Judging by how hot and intense it was now between him and Simone, it would only become more complicated if they actually did sleep together. So his instincts of self-preservation were screaming for him to stay away.

Maxwell wished the attraction between them was only physical. Then he could keep her in bed for hours having urgent sex until the desire for her body was out of his system. But the feeling in his gut told him it was far deeper. She was funny, sweet, and interesting, and she had a way of looking at him that made him feel ten feet tall. It would be too easy to fall hard for her. That was why he made the decision he did last night. If he did experience everything she had to offer, he honestly didn't know if he could just walk away a couple of days later. Maxwell also didn't want Simone to think that was all he was after.

Once out of the shower, he cleaned up with his shaver, then dressed in loose jeans and a white cotton shirt. He arrived at Simone's room a couple of minutes early, but she was ready to go, and looking as stunning as ever in stylish shorts and a tank top.

"So, what should we do today?" he asked her as they walked.

"I was thinking we could go into the city and walk around," she suggested. "I wouldn't mind doing a little shopping."

"Sounds good," Maxwell concurred.

They ate a light breakfast, then took a cab to the center of Montego Bay. From there, they spent several hours walking around. Simone found a few stores to browse through, including a boutique that sold handmade jewelry using rare precious stones. Their collection of amber with stunning, and she bought a pair of the earrings for her mother.

For lunch, Maxwell took her to a small off-the-path restaurant where they shared jerk chicken and fried fish while drinking ginger beer. It was a relaxed day, and they talked and laughed as though the night before had not happened. By midafternoon, they headed back to the resort with a plan to relax on the beach before dinner. Maxwell wanted to change into shorts, so Simone followed him back to his room.

Simone stood by the door of his suite as he took fresh clothes out of his suitcase and went into the bathroom. His windows faced the ocean and she eventually walked over to take a look. Maxwell approached her while she was standing on his balcony.

"This view is unbelievable, Maxwell!" she exclaimed.

"I know," he replied.

They stood beside each other and looked out over the beach and the ocean beyond. Simone pointed to a couple that flew by them parasailing.

"Have you ever done that?" she asked.

"A couple of times. It's fun. Do you want to try it?"

"I don't know. I'm not much of a thrill seeker."

"Really? That surprises me," he stated while looking at her speculatively. "You've done pretty well on our adventures so far."

"Well, I don't seem to be myself while I'm in Jamaica."

Maxwell shook his head and looked out over the water. "No, I think this is exactly who you really are. I think that people are more honest and true with strangers than people who know them well. They don't have to live up to other people's expectations or within the roles defined for them."

He could feel her eyes on his face, then felt her hand brush up his arm until it rested over his biceps.

"Is that also true for you?" she asked. "Are you being honest with me? Because I feel like I know you so well, like we've connected even though we are technically still strangers. Does that make sense?"

Maxwell covered her hand with his and let out a deep breath before replying, "It makes sense."

She stepped close to him to wrap both of her arms around his waist and laid her head against his chest. He did the same, pulling her into a tight hug.

"Let's enjoy being honest strangers," she whispered after several moments.

He pulled back to look into her face.

"Simone—"

He started to reiterate all the reasons they should not get closer, but she cut him off.

"I don't know what will happen after tomorrow, Maxwell, but I want to enjoy today, with you."

Her eyes revealed certainty and anticipation. Maxwell felt his heart start to beat at an accelerated rate. He could deny himself, but he had no willpower to deny her, not when she could express her desires so clearly.

"Simone, Simone . . ." he whispered into her hair before kissing her deeply and thoroughly.

Maxwell took her hand and led her into the room and stopped in front of the bed. There were no words needed as they removed their clothes until they were standing naked in front of each other.

Simone touched him first by trailing her fingers over the firm contour of his chest. He stood still, enjoying her exploration.

"I wanted to do this the first moment I saw you," she told him.

"Really?" he replied with a cocky grin. "So all this time, you've been lusting after my body!"

She grinned back, toying with his nipples. "That's right. I've been imagining all the things I would do to you."

"Oh yeah? Like what?"

One of her fingers began a lazy path down his stomach and played with the fine hairs down below. He sucked in a sharp breath while his eyes watched what she would do next.

"Like . . ." she continued in a soft, sexy voice, "I would rip off all your clothes."

"And then what?"

"Let's see, maybe . . . take you in my hands and caress every inch."

She wrapped her hand around the tip of his erection and demonstrated exactly what she meant.

His mouth went dry as he watched her handle his body with her delicate fingers.

"And maybe . . . I would slowly suck you into my mouth over and over again until you lose your mind."

Maxwell was aroused from the minute they

hugged on the balcony, but her words made him so hard he throbbed. All his intentions of slow, easy lovemaking evaporated in that instant.

"Simone, I think all that is going to have to wait."

He pulled her down onto the bed, rolling her until she was under him. He gently spread her legs so he could lie between them. On his knees, he reached for a condom inside the side table and rolled it on quickly. Then he looked down at her, completely open and flushed with desire for him. Their eyes met and clung as Maxwell entered her with one long stroke.

Deep, primal moans escaped both their throats.

Maxwell stilled for a moment, allowing her body to adjust to his size. She was wrapped around him like tight wet silk, threatening to squeeze the juice out of him before he was ready. He pulled out of her, then stroked back in to the hilt.

"Simone . . ." he uttered before he lost control.

Again and again, he delved into her sweet center with slow, long, sure strokes. Their groans became louder and sweat sprang out on their skin. He tried to prolong it, extend their connection, but the climax came to him too fast and hard to stop. He clenched his teeth tight, using all his willpower to hold it off. When it hit him, the strength of it was overpowering, causing his body to shake and quiver. Yet he continued to thrust deep, wanting Simone to join him in completion.

Seconds later, she came, screaming his name. He felt her flesh pulsating around him and smiled with satisfaction. They rode out the aftershocks still deeply connected.

When their bodies cooled and their breathing returned to normal, Maxwell tucked her under the sheets and left her for a few minutes. He returned with a wet towel, then proceeded to slowly wipe down her body. By the time he was done, they were both aroused again. This time, they took it slow, touching and teasing each other, and learning all the sweet spots.

When they came together again, Simone took control. Maxwell lay back and watched, allowing her the freedom to set their pace. She straddled him with her incredible legs and slowly encased his thick length inch by inch until she took him all. Then she started to ride him, her breasts bouncing with every gyration. It was the most erotic thing he had ever seen.

Simone started slow and smooth, telling him how good he felt inside her, and how much he filled her up. Maxwell could not keep still any longer. He ran his hand up her taut thigh and trailed his fingers over her fur-trimmed lips. She froze, anticipating more of his touch. Then he found the hot bud at her cleft and she went wild in her release, screaming with pleasure. Maxwell followed soon after.

At some point in the evening, they showered and went downstairs for dinner. They also took the walk along the beach that they had missed earlier in the day, and cuddled in a beach chair to watch the sun go down.

Maxwell gazed at Simone's profile as the sky turned golden, then fiery red. Tomorrow was Wednesday, probably the last day they would spend together before her girlfriend arrived.

He now realized that Simone was right. They should enjoy today for as long as it lasted. Who knew what would happen tomorrow? Maybe they could find a way to continue what they started on this island of paradise. Or maybe they would move on with separate lives and have only the memories of this rare thing between them.

The sun finally disappeared on the horizon. Simone looked at him in that moment, smiling with contentment. He smiled back.

The one thing he knew for sure was that he had no regrets, and would never forget her.

Chapter 8

Simone was waiting for Amy in the lobby when she arrived at the resort that afternoon. She was a tiny girl, no more than five feet and a couple of inches tall. Her curly blond hair was pulled into a casual ponytail, and her face was clean of makeup but showed signs of a tan.

"You're here!" exclaimed Simone when Amy swept through the doors.

"I made it, finally!" Amy replied, her blue eyes sparkling.

The girls hugged enthusiastically.

"Are you hungry? Do you want to get something to drink?" Simone asked her.

"No. I just want to go to the room and lie down for a minute. Then we're going to the beach."

Simone led her through the resort grounds and up to their suite.

"How was the flight?" she asked while they were walking.

"It was pretty smooth. But I couldn't shake the feeling that something else was going to happen and we would never get here."

"How's Cedric?"

"Fully recovered and feeling really bad about the whole thing. I told him it was okay, but he keeps saying he's ruined my wedding for me. But honestly, Moni, it's no big deal. I chose to get married at the resort so it wouldn't be a lot of work. But you know Cedric. He has to make a big deal out of everything.

"All I did was call the event planner and we went over the details on the phone. I have an appointment with her tomorrow morning, and that's it!"

"That sounds good," Simone added.

"Yeah. I even booked a spa visit on Friday to get our hair and nails done. So now we have the next two days to relax."

"Nice."

They entered their room and Simone showed her around. Amy quickly unpacked a few things, including her wedding dress.

"So, have you had a good time so far? What did you do with yourself?" asked Amy.

She had finally flopped back on her bed and kicked off her shoes. Simone sat in the chair near the desk.

"I've had fun. It's a really nice resort," she replied simply.

"I know. How's the food?"

"Really good, lots of choices."

Amy let out a deep breath, then jumped to her feet. "Okay, let's get some sun. Cedric's family has enough issues with me being white. I'm not going to show up at my wedding looking pale and pasty too."

The girls changed into their bathing suits and threw a few supplies into a couple of bags. The main part of the beach was pretty crowded and all the chairs were in use. They walked farther down to the edge of the hotel property until they reached a less crowded section. The sun was hot, but there was a soft breeze blowing in off the ocean. Simone and Amy reclined back in two chairs to relax.

"There was a picture of Kevin in the newspaper on Sunday," stated Amy after some time in silence. "Did you see it before you left?"

"No, I didn't. What for?" asked Simone.

He was often in the papers, either for charity or in the celebrity pages.

"I can't remember. Some gala dinner, I think."

"Oh, right. It was from last Thursday. I was supposed to go with him but I canceled," explained Simone.

"Well, he was with another girl in the picture."

Amy's statement hung in the air. Simone looked out at the water, and her lips turned up in a secret smile.

"I'm not surprised," she finally replied. "He was pretty pissed that I backed out at the last minute. We haven't spoken since."

"Simone, I've tried to keep my opinion to myself, but what do you see in that guy? He's so arrogant and you guys have nothing in common."

Simone shrugged. Amy was the only person she knew who didn't think Kevin Johnson was a woman's dream come true.

"We're just dating," Simone defended.

"Well, I hope you're not falling for him, 'cause I think you're wasting your time. I know he says he wants to get serious and all that, but give me a break. He's too in love with himself to care about anybody else. Look, you cancel one date with him and he just finds another girl!" She took a breath, then plunged on. "I know he's rich and famous, but none of that replaces love."

"Amy, we're just dating."

"Except you're not the type to just date, Simone. How many times have we had this conversation, and I'm the one trying to get you to go out with someone, give him a chance? Like that teacher I introduced you to, Paul. But you met him once and that was the end of it. No sparks, you said. I said 'get to know him, sometimes it takes time for the attraction to grow.' But, as usual, you insisted that you would feel it right away and just know.

"Well, Cedric and I have been together for over ten years and I can tell you, it's not always so clear. The right man doesn't just walk into your life with all the fireworks and everything works out perfect. Most of the time, you have to ask yourself if it should be so hard, and if it's all worth it. If you continue to say yes, then you know you have real love."

Simone looked out over the water, listening to Amy's words as they flowed through her tirade. There was no doubt that Amy knew what she was talking about. It could not be easy for her to be with a black man in Atlanta. Simone had personally witnessed the type of treatment and disrespect that they constantly faced. You really had to love someone to put up with all that.

She glanced over at her friend, knowing that Amy was really looking out for her.

"So I'm taking your advice, I'm trying to give someone a chance. And now you're telling me not to," Simone teased.

"Anyways! You never listen to me."

"I listen to everything you say, mommy Amy."

"Shut up! Stop calling me that!"

"Okay, mommy Amy."

Amy picked up a handful of sand and tossed it at

her. Simone jumped out of her chair to get out of the way, screaming loudly. The few people nearby looked over at them and watched as the tiny blond pixie chased the black Amazon right into the water.

They played in the waves for over an hour, then walked back to their chairs, exhausted. Stretched out again, they let the sun dry them off. Amy read a magazine, while Simone pretended to take a nap. Instead, her mind wandered to Maxwell. She speculated on what he was doing right now.

They had slept naked in each other's arms last night, and then wakened at dawn to have sex again. When they finally left his room, it was almost ten o'clock. They ate a quick breakfast and then Maxwell took her on a tour of Rose Hall, a large former plantation house not far from Montego Bay. As the legend goes, the matron of the house, a white woman named Annie Palmer, was a witch that killed all her husbands. In the end, she was killed by her own slaves.

They got back to the resort at around two o'clock, then spent a few minutes walking around the gardens. She was sitting under a coconut tree when he pulled a small, slender box out of his back pocket and put it in her hand. Simone was completely taken off guard. When she finally pulled off the lid, there was a stunning teardrop-shaped amber stone hanging from a delicate silver necklace.

"Oh, Maxwell. It's so beautiful," she exclaimed.

He took it out of the box and put it around her neck. "I got it while we were in Montego Bay yesterday. I knew right away that it was perfect for you."

She touched it gently, suddenly feeling emotional and teary.

"Something for you to remember me by," he added after a few minutes.

Simone stood up and stepped into his arms. They hugged tight, her face buried in the crook of his neck.

"Thank you. But I don't need anything to remember you by, Maxwell Harper," she whispered into his ear.

They stayed like that, tightly wrapped around each other, for a long time. Simone had to keep her eyes tightly squeezed so tears could not escape.

Eventually, they had to part and return to the hotel entrance so Simone could be there to meet Amy. Maxwell kissed her for the last time and left the resort in a taxi. She spent the next twenty minutes feeling completely alone, and trying to figure out a way for them to spend some more time together, even an hour.

"Are you hungry? I'm starving," Amy announced sometime later. "Let's head back."

As they trudged through the sand back toward the center of the resort, Simone glanced up at the hotel rooms that faced the beach. To her surprise, Maxwell stood on his balcony, looking down at her below. She stopped in her tracks, her heart in her throat.

"What's wrong?" Amy asked as she stopped beside her. "What are you looking at?"

Simone watched him walk back into the room, and he was gone by the time Amy's eyes swept over the area.

"Nothing," she finally replied, then continued the walk back.

Through dinner, the friends talked about going out dancing, trying to create a last-minute bachelorette party. There was a prewedding dinner planned for Thursday evening, so this was their only opportunity to have a wild time before the wedding. They intending to have a drink in the bar near the lobby, then walk to the resort next door to party in their nightclub. It was a great plan, but they ran out of energy even before leaving the restaurant, and ended up taking their drinks with them back to the room. Both girls were asleep before eleven o'clock.

Thursday sped by with a flurry of activities. They met with the resort event coordinator and went over every aspect of the wedding for Friday evening. Then they confirmed the intimate dinner that evening in one of the private dining rooms. After lunch, Amy dragged Simone down to the main swimming pool to play water polo and get some more sun. Simone protested that, unlike Amy, she had more than enough color, but Amy wasn't hearing it.

They were back in their suite with enough time for a nap before getting dressed for dinner.

"Are you nervous?" Simone asked Amy as they shared the counter in the bathroom.

"A little. I don't know why, though. I see Cedric's parents all the time and I think they have finally accepted me. Everything is going to be fine."

"Everything will be perfect," added Simone.

Amy smiled, but it seemed shaky.

"It's not me I'm worried about," she continued. "Cedric's family is a little weird. They have all these issues among each other. I've asked Cedric about it but he just dismisses it as nothing. I just don't want to deal with it, you know?"

"I can imagine."

"Now, to top it off, Cedric's older brother will be there. He's our best man. And that's a whole other story. He's like the black sheep of the family, and Cedric's dad is not thrilled about it."

"Wow," Simone said. "That does sound like a lot of issues. But don't worry. I'm sure they wouldn't do anything to ruin this for you and Cedric. Like I said, it's going to be perfect."

The private dining room they had was part of one of the restaurants, but partitioned off by sliding doors. It had full-length windows overlooking the beach. They tilted open, allowing the ocean air to flow in.

Amy and Simone got there a few minutes before seven. The staff was setting the table to seat ten people, and soft reggae was playing in the background. Cedric and his parents arrived several minutes later. It was immediately clear he got his looks from his father. Both men were around five feet ten inches and had the same walnut complexion and wide, thick features. His mother was a more rich brown tone and her facial bones were finely sculpted. Amy hugged them, then introduced Simone to her future in-laws, Thomas and Dolores Smith. A server walked by and handed them a glass of rum punch.

"Are you enjoying Jamaica so far, Simone?" asked Mrs. Smith.

Amy and Cedric were a few steps away talking to three other guests who had just walked in, leaving Simone with the older couple.

"Yes, ma'am. It's incredibly beautiful," she replied.

"Cedric told us that you've been here by yourself since Sunday. Did you get to leave the resort?" Mr. Smith inquired.

"I did, actually. I walked around Montego Bay, and went to see Rose Hall."

"That's nice. It's not really safe for a woman to wander around alone. Cedric should have told his cousins you were here. I'm sure one of them would have taken you around, maybe shown you some of the countryside," Mr. Smith suggested.

"Actually," Simone replied, "I was able to go on a road trip. We drove along the coast and through Ocho Rios."

"That's lovely. So you went to Dunn's River Falls?" his wife chimed in.

Simone shook her head while sipping her drink. "No. Unfortunately, we didn't stop. We went south to a beautiful valley filled with orange and banana trees."

"Really?" asked Mrs. Smith, her interest suddenly piqued. "In which parish?"

"Oh, I'm sorry. I'm not sure. But the town was called Gold Mine."

Mr. and Mrs. Smith looked at each other, clearly surprised. Simone looked back and forth between them, smiling politely but curious about their reactions.

"Oh no, dear," said Mrs. Smith. "You must be mistaken. Gold Mine is a tiny little place."

"I'm pretty sure, and it was quite small," she insisted.

Mrs. Smith shook her head.

"I'm from Gold Mine," she told Simone in a patient but firm voice. "That could not be where you went. It's not even on a map."

"Maybe she means Golden Head. That's near Ochie, isn't it?" her husband suggested.

"No, no. There's no valley in Golden Head. She must mean Golden Grove."

Simone decided not to argue with them, and listened politely as they debated which town Simone was actually referring to.

She was just thinking about the odds of meeting

someone else from Gold Mine, when all three of them turned toward a slight commotion near the door. Cedric was hugging a tall man, and they were both laughing with joy. When they broke apart, Simone found herself staring at Maxwell Harper.

Chapter 9

Simone almost dropped her glass. Their eyes met immediately and she could see he was shocked also. He looked so handsome in a light gray suit and soft blue shirt, open at the collar to reveal some of that lean chest that she was so familiar with. She turned away and put her glass on the dining room table, not sure of what to do. Her hand went right to the amber necklace around her neck.

When she turned back, Mrs. Smith was hugging Maxwell tightly around his waist. He gently patted her back.

"Hello, Mom," she heard him say.

He gave a stiff nod to Mr. Smith, who responded with an awkward bow forward.

"Simone," called Amy with a wave of her hand, beckoning her.

When she reached them, the other relatives had walked away with Cedric's parents, leaving only Amy, Cedric, and Maxwell.

"Simone, this is Cedric's brother, Maxwell."

Still not sure how best to handle the situation, Simone just smiled. She avoided looking into his face, afraid of what it would reveal. What if he pretended he didn't know her?

"Simone and I have met," she heard him announce in a strong voice.

She met his eyes then, and they were black and intense. Silence followed his statement as Amy and Cedric looked between them, trying to understand what Maxwell meant.

"How?" demanded Amy in a high voice.

"Here on the resort," Simone replied. "He was kind enough to help me after a slight mishap."

"What? What happened?" Amy asked.

"It was nothing! I just slipped by the pool and fell in. Maxwell came to my rescue."

"Wow!" Cedric added, still looking back and forth between Simone and his brother. "What a coincidence. When was this?"

"Sunday," Maxwell told him.

"Sunday?" repeated Cedric. "You've been here since Sunday? I thought you were arriving today?"

Maxwell just shrugged, clearly not feeling obligated to explain himself.

One of the waiters approached Amy at that moment and suggested they start dinner. Simone, Maxwell, and Cedric went to the table while Amy went around the room to let the other guests know. As they each picked a spot, Cedric introduced Simone to his other relatives, his aunt Rosette and uncle Dennis on his mom's side, then their daughter, Michelle, and her husband, Calvin.

Once they were all seated, the meal went smoothly, with everyone being polite and in good spirits. Most of the conversation was by the older couples, talking about Jamaican politics and economics. Simone was beside Amy on her right and Uncle Dennis on her left while Cedric was across from Amy with Maxwell

on his left. There were too many people between
them for Maxwell and Simone to talk to each other.

"Why didn't you tell me you met Maxwell?" demanded Amy in a low voice.

"I didn't know who he was," Simone replied defensively.

"Still, you didn't mention meeting anyone," she
shot back between bites of her meal. "What happened between you two?"

"What?"

"Oh, please. Don't tell me nothing happened. I
saw the way he looked at you," Amy shot back in an
excited voice a little louder than she intended.

A few people looked at them, including Cedric
and Maxwell.

Amy cleared her throat.

"Tell me later," she demanded and went back
to eating and listening to the other talk.

Simone continued to eat and tried to keep her
eyes on her plate or on the table. She was completely flustered and thrown. Tons of thoughts
were racing through her mind as she tried to remember the details of their conversation over the
last few days.

Why hadn't he told her he was in Jamaica for a
wedding? They probably would have figured
things out pretty quickly if he had. Why didn't he
tell his brother, or the rest of his family, that he
had been here for almost a week? Why did he and
Cedric have different last names?

Simone then remembered Amy's comment
about their family issues. Maxwell was the black
sheep she had referred to, and his father was not
happy that he was Cedric's best man. What a sad
situation, she thought to herself.

She could not resist glancing toward Maxwell.
He was about a head taller than his younger

brother, so she could clearly see his face, and he
was relaxed back in his chair looking right at her.
Simone smiled a little and he nodded back. Her
heart raced and she was suddenly more excited
than she had been since they parted yesterday.
Maxwell was going to be Amy's brother-in-law, regardless of the other family problems. Maybe they
wouldn't have to go their separate ways after all.
Maybe they could have more than a vacation fling.

They had just been served the final course of the
meal, a mango mousse cake, when Mr. Smith stood
to make a toast. His voice was quiet and low.

"I would like to say a few words from my wife,
Dolores, and me." He cleared his throat. "Cedric,
we have always been proud of you and your decisions in life. As a boy, you were the best son a
father could ask for. And now you have become
the man we raised you to be—ambitious, proud,
respectful, and responsible. Tomorrow, you will be
a husband and head of your household. In time,
a father with children of your own, God willing.

"Amy, Dolores and I were not always supportive
of your relationship with our son. We wanted to
save you both from the hardships that will probably always be there and that your children will face.
But Cedric has made his choice and we respect it
as the right one for him. We welcome you into our
family."

Simone quickly glanced at Amy to see how she
would react. She was looking at Cedric and her
face didn't show any emotion.

Mr. Smith picked up his glass, and everyone
picked theirs up also and stood.

"To Cedric and Amy," he announced and raised
the glass. The others followed suit.

Simone's eyes met Maxwell's as they sat back
down. His were hot and his jaw was clenched in a

hard line. It was the first time she had seen any sign of anger or hostility in him. She had to fight the urge to go over and pull him into her arms.

The group lingered around the dining room table until almost nine o'clock. Maxwell was the first to leave. Cedric spoke with him in whispered tones for a few minutes, and then Maxwell stood up.

"Good evening," he stated, then walked out of the room.

Everyone was silent as they watched him leave.

"Still the same arrogant bastard!" muttered Mr. Smith.

His wife shot him a sharp look and placed a restraining hand on his lower arm. Amy and Cedric looked at each other, but no one said anything else for a couple of minutes.

The gathering ended soon after.

"Cedric is staying with his aunt and uncle until after the wedding," Amy explained to Simone. "His parents are there too, so he's going to leave with them now. I'm going to walk them out to the lobby."

"Okay," replied Simone. "I'll wait for you in our room."

"What do you want to do tonight?"

"I don't know. It's your last night as a single woman, so you decide," said Simone.

"To be honest, I wouldn't mind just relaxing and watching whatever is on television," Amy admitted, sounding embarrassed by her lack of enthusiasm. "I'm sorry."

"Don't be sorry," insisted Simone with a dismissive wave of her hand. "I'm fine with whatever you want. I'm a little tired myself."

"Okay."

The two girls hugged.

"Thanks for being such a good friend, Simone," Amy added.

Simone said good-bye to everyone and watched them go. On her way out, she stopped in the bathroom for a few minutes before leaving the restaurant. Maxwell was waiting for her outside, leaning casually against the wall. His suit jacket was thrown over his shoulder and hooked by one finger. She walked up to him.

"Hi," she said.

He stepped in front of her and kissed her hard, and long. When he finally released her, she was breathless. They looked at each other in the night's light.

"I guess you won't be able to get rid of me after all," she added, using humor to hide her shyness.

Maxwell took her hand and started walking in the direction of the rooms. He still didn't speak.

"Are you okay?" she asked softly once the silence became unbearable.

"I'm all right," he replied, but his voice had a biting edge that she was not familiar with.

They ended up back at their spot, in the garden next to the secluded pool. He stepped to the back of a large bird-of-paradise tree so they could not be seen by anyone who passed by. His jacket was tossed on a thick bush beside them. With his back leaned against the tree, he pulled her into another hard kiss. Simone responded, teasing him with her lips. She felt his thick arousal between them.

"I missed you last night," he finally said. "I couldn't sleep."

His mouth was on hers again, sucking and stroking her tongue.

"I missed you too," she groaned. "I didn't think I would ever see you again."

"Come back to my room with me."

He sucked hard on her neck, causing her to squirm with delight.

"I can't. Amy's going to be waiting for me in our room."

"Tell her you went for a walk."

He was now circling her ear with his tongue. His hands were up her skirt and cupping and squeezing her cheeks.

"Mmmm . . ." she moaned and pressed her mouth on his chest, drawing a wet trail down the center. "I can't. She'll get worried."

"Just a few minutes . . ."

Simone's eyes widened with surprise as he deftly peeled down her panties and slipped them into his pants pocket. Then he was kissing her again and running hot hands over her naked bum.

"God, you feel so good," he uttered. "I can't keep my hands off you."

He slid his hands lower, his fingers searching for the center of her arousal. They explored her slick quivering flesh until one slid in deep.

"So wet," he moaned into her ear while his fingers stroked at her.

"Maxwell, this is crazy," she whispered, almost panting.

"I know, I know. You make me crazy."

He didn't stop, and Simone really didn't want him to. This was madness, but she didn't care. She was already lost in the sensations he created and fighting hard not to scream.

With the last of her control, Simone undid his pants and took his hot erection into her hands. Its size filled her palm and jumped at her stroking touch. She felt him shiver with pleasure.

There they stayed, hidden behind an exotic tree, locked in an erotic embrace, giving and receiving pleasure until they reached delicious release.

Chapter 10

The wedding was a beautiful ceremony set outside on a grassy hill overlooking the water and against the setting sun.

Cedric and Maxwell looked very handsome in their cream suits, and Simone was stunning in her simple silk dress the color of aged champagne. Amy took everyone's breath away as she walked down the aisle between linen-covered chairs. She wore a long white satin gown, cut straight with a slit up the back. The bodice was strapless and studded with white pearls. It was the perfect choice for her slight frame, blond hair, and now tanned skin.

There was plenty of food, drink, and music for the small group of about twenty guests, all family or close friends of Cedric and his parents.

Even Maxwell had to admit he was having a good time. It was nice to see the aunts, uncles, and cousins that still lived in Jamaica. He would have liked to talk more with his mother, but his father hovered around her like a hawk. Maxwell didn't want to risk a confrontation that could ruin the evening.

His only regret was that he couldn't hang out more with his brother.

Last night, while still restless after he had walked Simone back to her room, Maxwell had called Cedric on his cell phone and met him at a local bar in Montego Bay. They spent a few hours talking.

"I'm proud of you too, Cedric," Maxwell told him at one point.

They were sitting on an outdoor patio holding their second bottles of cold Red Stripe beer. Several Jamaicans were playing a popular board game called Ludi.

Cedric looked at him with sadness in his eyes. He knew that Maxwell was referencing the speech their father had given at dinner. Both felt that the intent of the words had not been to praise Cedric, but to insult Maxwell.

"Why is that?" Cedric asked.

"Because you stood your ground in your own way. Last I heard, Pop was doing everything in his power to make sure you and Amy did not stay together."

Cedric looked down at the ground.

"So he said," he replied. "But once I moved out from under his roof, what could he do? You know how he is. His bark is worse than his bite. I just ignore his blustering. Mom's always liked Amy anyway."

Maxwell nodded. He had met his new sister-in-law for the first time yesterday, but had heard only good things about her from his mom and Cedric over the last few years. He was glad that his brother had found such a special woman.

"Yeah, I know how he is," Maxwell reiterated.

"I'm really happy you came, though. It wouldn't have been the same without you, man," Cedric added.

"I wouldn't have missed it for the world."

They drank their beers, both wrapped in their thoughts.

"I can't believe you and Pop haven't spoken for

almost nine years," Cedric finally declared, unable to stay away from the topic at the center of the family drama.

Maxwell shrugged.

"I think he said everything he needed to say the night I left," Maxwell told him softly.

"Come on, man! You know he was just blowing hot air like he always does. He didn't mean anything he said."

"No, Cedric. He meant every word. I know it and he knows it. Even Mom knows it. You're the only one who wants to believe that he treated you and me the same."

Cedric looked at his brother, the man he had looked up to his whole life, and didn't know what to say. His family had been torn apart so many years ago, and this was the first time he had the nerve to talk to Maxwell about it.

"Anyway, it's old news now. Leaving Atlanta was the best thing I ever did," continued Maxwell.

"It all seems so ridiculous now anyway," said Cedric. "By the time April had her baby that fall, everyone knew that Bobby Donaldson was the real father, not you."

"Yeah, well, that girl is pure evil. Aunt Helen must be rolling in her grave knowing her daughter turned out like that."

"You knew the baby wasn't yours, didn't you?"

"It couldn't have been. I never slept with April."

Maxwell's statement was made with emotionless certainty. Cedric's jaw dropped.

He remembered the climactic events as if it were yesterday. His dad's sister, Helen, had died from liver problems and her sixteen-year-old daughter, April, had come from Detroit to live with them in Atlanta. Cedric was also sixteen at the time and

Maxwell was twenty-two. One day, after she had been with them for about six months, Pop came home from work early and found April naked in Maxwell's bedroom. Two days later, she told everyone she was pregnant and Maxwell was the father.

"Cedric, she was my cousin and she was a kid. I would never go there."

"Not your real cousin," he shot back, still shocked.

Maxwell blew out a deep breath. It was true; April was not his real cousin since Thomas Smith was not his real father. It was the fact at the heart of it all. "Still, she was just sixteen. I was a grown man."

Cedric made a deep scoffing noise in his throat. "Bobby Donaldson was only a year younger than you."

"That's on him, man."

"Why didn't you just tell everyone you hadn't slept with her?" Cedric persisted.

"I did, Cedric, but Pop didn't believe me. I told him that I had just gotten out of the shower and found April in my room without her top on. He called me a dirty bastard liar and slapped me across the face. I punched him in the nose, and it went downhill from there."

"He said April was naked on the bed."

"Well, that's what he wanted Mom to believe," Maxwell told him, unable to keep some of the old bitterness out of his voice. "Anyway, you heard what he had to say when I tried to confront April and convince her to tell the truth a few days later. He said I was a dirty rutting dog like my father and he should have left me in Jamaica to beg on the streets."

The words faded away in the warm night air, but the impact lingered within both men.

Maxwell had left his mother's house that night, then come back the next day while everyone was out. He only took the bare necessities, not wanting to keep anything given to him by that man. He kept in touch with his mom, and when the job in Toronto came through, he met her at a restaurant near her workplace to say good-bye. He hadn't been back to Atlanta since.

Now, as Maxwell looked over at Cedric dancing with his new bride in the night under the flickering light of lanterns, he wished he hadn't stayed away so long. In the beginning, it was anger, bitterness, and youth that made him stay away. Then it became hardened stubbornness. But Cedric had done nothing to deserve his big brother walking out of his life. It was his one real regret in the whole mess.

Maxwell's eyes then found Simone sitting and talking with his cousin, Michelle. The sight of her caused a tingle to run down to the base of his stomach. He now had another reason to visit Atlanta.

As though feeling his gaze, Simone glanced over at him. Even though they were yards apart, he could see the disappointment on her face. Michelle looked over also, then leaned close to Simone, her mouth working. Simone looked away from him, and Maxwell cursed under his breath. Clearly, he was the topic of their conversation, and he knew exactly what family gossip his cousin had been sharing.

Maxwell went to the bar and ordered a hard drink, knocking it back with one long swallow. He flicked his wrist to request another, though he savored it for a little while longer. The third glass of rum was still in his hands when the new bride and groom were ready to make their exit from the party. Everyone hugged Cedric and Amy as they left to start their weeklong honeymoon in a room of their own on the resort. Maxwell was the last person they spoke to.

The two brothers clasped each other tight, exchanging promises to stay in touch and see each other soon. Maxwell kissed Amy on the cheek and welcomed her to their family as his new sister.

The other guests slowly took their leave soon after. Maxwell kept his eyes on Simone as she walked around on Amy's behalf to make sure all the final details were taken care of. He then walked toward her as she struggled to get a handhold on all the wedding gifts.

"Let me help you with those," he offered, taking several of them out of her arms.

"Thank you," she replied politely.

"Where to?"

"Just inside the hall." She gestured to a building nearby. "There is a locked storage room that they have given Amy for the rest of the week."

Maxwell followed her, then helped her put all the items away.

They stood awkwardly beside each other for a few seconds.

"Did you enjoy the wedding?" he finally asked.

"It was beautiful," she replied, giving him a tight smile.

Maxwell nodded in agreement.

"You looked beautiful," he added while his eyes roamed over her face.

They settled on the amber necklace that reached just below her collarbone. It looked perfect with her dress and against the tone of her skin.

Simone looked down at it also, then ran her fingers over the smooth stone.

"So, what now?" Maxwell asked.

He was referring to the rest of the night, but knew right away that she could think he was asking about this thing between them. He was about to clarify it, but Simone looked away from him to some point off in the distance.

"I don't know," she said simply.

She then turned and made her way back to the grassy hill where the ceremony had been held. Only the hotel staff remained, cleaning up. Maxwell followed behind her as she continued on down the path that led to the hotel lobby. Neither spoke. He wanted to demand that she talk to him, tell him what had her acting so cold, but he didn't.

His patience ran out about ten minutes later. He took her arm, forcing her to stop walking and look at him. She pulled away, as though afraid. That hit him like a punch in his stomach.

They stood, staring at each other.

"Say it," he demanded in a quiet but hard voice. Simone flinched at his tone.

"What?" she demanded, clearly confused.

"Say what you have to say."

"I don't know what you're talking about, Maxwell."

He clenched his teeth hard. The liquor now flowed through his blood, adding fuel to his disappointment.

"Then let me help you," he snapped sarcastically. "Say, Thanks for the tour of Jamaica and the good times, but it's time to say good-bye."

"What?"

"Isn't that what you've been trying to find a way to tell me? Ever since you found out that I'm the sick bastard that knocked up my sixteen-year-old cousin?"

Simone's eyes widened and he knew right away that she had been told.

"Maxwell—"

He cut her off.

"Here, I'll do it for you, save you the trouble.

Thank you, Simone, for the really hot sex, but it's time to move on."

She slapped him hard across his face.

Maxwell looked back at her with a nasty smile. If he wasn't a little drunk, he would see that she regretted it right away.

"Maxwell, that's not what I want to say at all. I was just . . ."

She reached out a hand to touch his arm, but he shrugged it away and walked past her without a word.

"Maxwell!"

He kept moving even though he could hear her footsteps following him.

"Don't walk away like this. Let's talk about it. Tell me what really happened."

When he did stop, it was so sudden that she almost crashed into him. Her eyes were pleading, but he looked straight into them and spoke to her with disgust.

"Remember what I told you. Strangers are honest with each other, Simone. You trusted me with your life when you only knew my name. Now you've met my family and they've told you who they think I am. Suddenly you don't want to be anywhere near me. We should have stayed strangers."

"No, that's not true. Maxwell!"

He walked away with long, angry strides.

Chapter 11

"Folks, it's about that time again. It's eleven fifty-five on a beautiful Thursday morning, and we're about to start the Rare Groove hour here on GROOVE FM 99.1. Remember to listen in at twelve thirty for the B-Side Contest. We'll play a song from the B side of your favorite vinyl. The first caller who can tell us the artist and the name of the song will win a hundred-dollar gift certificate to Eye Candy Clothing Store.

"Right now we'll end this hour with 'Rumors' by Timex Social Club, on GROOVE FM 99.1."

Simone switched off the mic and Michael ran the music. She prepped for the next hour, but her mind was a hundred miles away.

She had returned from Jamaica almost two weeks ago, and still the feelings of sadness and heartache pressed down on her. It hurt just as much as it did the night Maxwell walked away from her and out of her life. She had called to him, tried to catch up with him, but he had just kept going. Tears had been streaming down her face. Even now, just thinking about it brought a lump to her throat.

When it was clear that he was not going to come

back, Simone went to their spot in the garden to wait for him, knowing he would have to pass there on the way to his room. She sat in the dark for over an hour, then finally gave up and dragged herself to her room. The next morning, after only four hours of sleep, Simone was knocking on his door by seven o'clock. There was no answer.

The front desk told her he had already checked out.

Michael pulled her out of her thoughts, indicating it was time to go back on air. She continued her show on autopilot.

"Are you sure you're okay, Moni?" asked Michael as they walked together to the parking lot.

She smiled, trying to reassure him again. "I'm fine, really."

"That's what you've been saying since your vacation, but you don't look it," he told her. "You were supposed to rest for a week, not come back more tired."

Simone knew he was really worried about her, and was trying to make her laugh. She gave him a brighter smile. "I'm okay really. I just have a few things on my mind, that's all."

Michael accepted her answer reluctantly and they went to their cars.

Simone didn't go home right away. She was having dinner with Kevin that evening and wanted something new to wear, so she headed to her favorite clothing store. They had met for drinks last week, seeing each other for the first time since before her trip.

She had waited until she was back in Atlanta to return his message. When she called him that Sunday evening, he had not been pleased. Simone just gave him some excuse about not having her cell phone on during the holiday. He questioned her more, but she didn't explain further, nor did she really care what he thought.

Between Saturday, her last day on the island spent alone, and her flight back on Sunday, Simone had decided to stop seeing Kevin. She tried to tell herself that it was for all the valid reasons that Amy had stated. They didn't have anything in common, and she didn't want to date someone just because he was the man she should want to be with. But deep down, she knew it was because of Maxwell. She had felt that spark for the first time in her life, and she couldn't imagine a relationship with another man without that kind of passion.

Simone had agreed to meet Kevin for drinks last week to break things off, but she never got the chance. Kevin spent the whole time talking about all the things going on his life so that she couldn't even start the conversation she wanted to have. Then, when he dropped her home, he gave her a wrapped jewelry box followed by a deep kiss. They were interrupted by his cell phone, so Simone took the opportunity to leave his car while he talked on the phone.

The box had contained a stunning diamond bracelet.

Now, as she reached her apartment carrying a couple of new outfits, she admitted to herself that she had no clue what to do.

Kevin was picking her up at seven, so she had almost two hours to get ready. She went into the bathroom and filled the tub. Her body was still soaking in soothing bubbles when the phone rang. It was her friend Maya.

"Hey, girl," Maya said brightly. "Did you find something to wear?"

"Yeah," replied Simone.

"You're going to love Mitchell's Restaurant. Natasha said she saw one of the Falcons' players there just last week."

"Really?" she replied without any real interest.

Natasha was their other close friend, and all three of them had met in their freshman year at Morehouse as journalism majors. They had stayed close, doing almost everything together for the last ten years.

"But I'm sure you're used that by now. Kevin knows so many people," Maya continued. "So, I guess things are going well with you guys, huh?"

"Hmm," replied Simone, not wanted to say anything to her one way or the other.

Simone had met Kevin at the radio station when he joined her show to do an interview. He asked for her phone number afterward. Since then, her friends had been acting as though she had won the lottery. She had tried to tell both Natasha and Maya that she found him a little boring and self-centered, but they just went on and on about what a catch he was and how many women would give their right arm to be with him.

Now, almost three months later, they were his biggest admirers even though neither had even met him yet. It wasn't that they were shallow or gold diggers. Natasha was a junior editor at the *Atlanta Daily World*, and Maya had a great job with an investment firm. They just knew how hard it was to find a good man. Most of the women she knew thought Kevin Johnson was the ideal image of the man they should marry. Successful, charismatic, ambitious, and able to take care of them financially.

None of those things had ever been important to Simone. All she ever wanted was a man who loved her and whom she loved in return. A man that made her heart beat whenever she saw him and made her feel safe in his arms. Everything else was secondary.

But what do you do when you finally find that man and he walks out of your life without looking back?

"Well," Maya continued, not noticing Simone's lack of enthusiasm, "my hairstylist was telling me that his friend had a friend that works with Kevin's publicist. And apparently Kevin has been talking about a new woman in his life that he wants to get serious with."

"Really?" she replied, her voice flat.

"Simone, did you hear what I said? Kevin is telling people that you are the one!"

"How do you know he's talking about me? Apparently he was in the paper with another woman just two weeks ago. I'm sure I'm not the only one he's dating."

"I'm sure she was just a fill-in. You did cancel on him last minute, and he couldn't exactly go to an event like that without a date. The plate was already paid for," Maya surmised. "Anyway, I'm sure it's you. Didn't he just give you an expensive diamond bracelet? I'm telling you, if this continues the way things are going, you guys will be engaged by the end of the year."

Simone rolled her eyes. "Maya, we've just gone out a few times. We haven't even slept together yet."

"Are you serious? Well, that confirms it! A man like him isn't going to wait weeks to get some unless he has plans. He must get it thrown at him every day."

"I'm sure he does, but I just don't feel that way about him," Simone finally told her. "I told you before, there's something missing there. We've kissed, we've messed around a bit, but I honestly don't think it can go beyond that."

"You know what you need? You guys need to go away, maybe to one of those spa retreats. You could wear some of the sexy lingerie you love to buy and I'm sure—"

Simone cut her off. "Sorry, Maya, I just noticed the time. I have to run or I'm going to be late for dinner. I'll see you tomorrow, okay?"

She ended the call and reclined in the soapy water.

Kevin arrived thirty minutes late, and called her from downstairs. When she got to the car, his brother, Donald, was in the passenger seat. Simone slid into the back wordlessly.

At the restaurant, they were joined by three other people: two of Kevin's friends and one of their girlfriends. Simone sat between Kevin and the girl-friend, whose name was Trinity. It was a pleasant enough evening with the men joking among them-selves, leaving the girls to talk to each other. Trinity was a senior at Howard University and turned out to be pretty nice. Simone could tell it was her first time out at such an expensive restaurant. Her eyes widened with shock as she looked over the menu.

Kevin paid for everything, as usual, even though his brother and friends drank most of the alcohol. Simone was surprised when he dropped Donald off at the condo they shared, then drove her home. He parked the car and walked her upstairs. She invited him in, thinking it would be the per-fect opportunity to talk.

The minute the door closed, Kevin was all over her. Simone was so surprised at first that she stood still for several seconds. His lips pressed on hers and his tongue pried her mouth open. She felt nothing except invaded and vulnerable.

When his hand grasped her breast through her top, she pulled her away from his and tried to step back. Kevin squeezed her harder, trying to pinch her nipple.

"Kevin," she protested.

He ignored her, reaching under her top to fondle her through her bra.

"Let's go into the bedroom," he suggested.

"Kevin, I need to talk to you," Simone stated, trying again to step away.

"Later," was his reply, holding her close with his grip on her butt. He then slapped one of the cheeks while grinning at her.

Simone was suddenly very annoyed. She broke away from him and walked into her living room.

"What's the problem?" he asked as he followed her. "I'm just playing with you. You now how much I love your ass."

"Kevin, I think you should go."

"Oh, come on, Simone. Don't you think it's time to stop playing hard to get?"

"Hard to get?" she repeated. "Is that what you think I'm doing?"

"I know that you're not the type of girl that's going to jump in bed right away. Haven't I been the perfect gentleman? I've been patient, but now it's time to give some of it up. I think I deserve a little taste, that's all I'm saying," he told her.

His expression said he thought this was a perfectly reasonable request.

Simone shook her head, torn between disgust and anger.

"Like I said, it's time for you to go," she stated simply.

Kevin looked shocked, like those words had never been said to him before. "You're serious!"

She didn't reply, just walked over to the door.

"Okay, I get it, I rushed too fast," he stated, still standing in the living room. "I'm sorry, baby. It's just that you look so hot tonight and I've wanted you for so long. Come on, don't be like that. Look, we'll forget the whole thing. We can wait until it's right for you."

She looked at him skeptically, surprised at how quickly he turned on the charm. He walked over to her and gently stroked her arms. "Let's get together on Saturday and we'll spend the whole evening together, just the two of us."

Simone wanted him gone from her apartment, so she relaxed her shoulders and nodded.

"That's my girl," he said, then pressed a hard kiss on her lips. "I'll call you tomorrow."

Finally, he left and Simone closed the door hard behind him. She stood there for long minutes, her arms wrapped around her waist, fighting the lump that was growing in her throat. In that moment she felt so alone, wanting Maxwell more than ever before. She missed everything about him, his touch, his smell, even the sound of his voice. Most of all, she missed the incredible feeling of being safe in his hands.

She finally went to her bedroom and spent another night crying herself to sleep.

Chapter 12

Another week passed and very little changed for Simone.

Kevin was clearly trying to make up for his behavior that evening in her apartment. He arranged for an intimate evening together on Saturday as promised, and even spent time talking to her rather than on his cell phone. A few nights later, she also went with him to a very exclusive party thrown by a local record label. He stayed by her side the whole time, and introduced her as his girlfriend. Simone felt numb and floated through the whole thing, but his efforts made her hold off on her plans to break up with him.

That weekend, Amy called Simone to say she had printed off some of the pictures from the wedding. They arranged to meet on Saturday afternoon for lunch at a restaurant near Amy and Cedric's place a few minutes away from Buckhead. She and Amy had spoken a few times since Amy's return from her honeymoon. With every conversation, Simone wanted to ask about Maxwell, but could not seem to get the words out. She had admitted to Amy while they were in Jamaica that she

found Maxwell attractive, but never revealed how
much time they had spent together, or how intimate they had become.

Then, as the girlfriends sat eating and flipping
through the stack of glossy photos, Simone found
a picture of her and Maxwell standing beside each
other as best man and maid of honor. The flood-
gates opened.

"Amy, I have to tell you something," she started,
then poured out the whole story, only withholding
the most intimate details. Simone ended with the
rumor of him sleeping with his young cousin, and
their confrontation after the wedding.

"It wasn't true, Simone," Amy interjected. "He
never touched his cousin. She got pregnant from
some guy in the neighborhood and tried to trap
Maxwell into being the father. I've met April, and
I can tell you that's exactly the type of thing she
would do, even at sixteen."

"I screwed up, Amy. I should have just told him
what his cousin had said and let him explain," admitted Simone.

"Simone, unfortunately, Cedric and Maxwell
come from a pretty screwed-up family situation. I'm
sure his reaction had more to do with dealing with
Cedric's dad than with you. Trust me, that man can
drive anyone crazy."

"Deep down, I knew it couldn't be true, but I
hesitated, wondering if I had made a big mistake
getting so close to someone that I really didn't
know. He was so angry."

Amy let out a deep breath in sympathy. "Don't
blame yourself, Simone. It's understandable how
you felt. Even Cedric believed Maxwell had slept
with April, and he loves his brother and looks up
to him. Now he's pretty broken up about believing

his father and assuming that Maxwell was capable of that kind of thing."

"Amy, I knew in my heart it wasn't true even while Michelle was going on and on about it. But I got scared. How could I fall for a man and get so close to him so soon? What did I really know about him?"

"Well, right now you know him better than anyone, and I'm married to his brother. Cedric only tells me stories of how close they were as kids, and his parents never speak his name."

Simone looked at the picture again.

"What are you going to do?" Amy asked finally.

"I don't know."

"Call him," her friend suggested simply. "Cedric has his number. Call him."

"And say what?"

"It doesn't matter. But you're going to be miserable if you don't at least try."

Maxwell was struggling with the same decision. With every day that passed, it became harder to reach out to Simone. He had been listening to her radio show on the Internet every day since his return home. For five hours in the middle of his workday, he smiled at her dry humor and was amazed by her ability to draw in her audience. It should have been easy to send her an e-mail, or just call the station, but he didn't do it. What words could he use to explain his unforgivable behavior after his brother's wedding? How could he tell her how much he regretted his harsh words and walking away from her the way he had done?

His anger had faded quickly that night, and he regretted his actions immediately. He then spent a long time at the hotel bar getting sober and thinking about the decisions in his life. By six thirty the next morning, he was standing in front of Simone's door trying to find the courage to apologize to her before he left for the airport. But, in the end, he did the only thing he knew how to do: he walked away again.

Now, three weeks later, it wasn't any easier. Maxwell listened to her sweet voice during the day, and dreamed about her at night. Sometimes, in his unconscious mind, they just talked while holding hands, their words an unintelligible murmer that didn't matter. But most times, their bodies were hot and wet with sweat, meshed in one of many different sexual positions. The images were so real and vividly hot that he woke up pulsingly hard and with the taste of her still on his lips.

It was Tuesday afternoon, and Maxwell was in his office in downtown Toronto. He was a project manager for a well-established engineering firm, and his team was currently working on a proposal to reinforce an old city bridge. As was his routine, Maxwell listened to GROOVE FM on his laptop while he worked. There were a few minutes left on Simone's show.

"Well, folks, it's time to say to good-bye," she told her audience. "I hope you enjoyed our time together on the Midday Joyride. You're listening to Moni S on Groove FM 99.1, and I'm going to leave you with a song from one of my favorite artists. It goes out to the stranger I'm missing. Here is the prince of neo-soul, Maxwell, with 'Ascension' from the *Urban Hanging Suite* album."

Maxwell stopped chewing and looked at the computer screen, not sure he had heard what he thought he had heard. He was still staring forward with a goofy gaze when his coworker Amar Shah came into the room.

"What's going on?" Amar asked after a while when Maxwell still did not acknowledge his presence.

"What?" Maxwell asked.

The song was still playing and he had been focused on every word.

"Nothing, man. I came to see if you found those specs from that job in Woodbridge last week."

"Oh, uh . . . yeah. It's right here," replied Maxwell.

He swung around on his chair and handed Amar one of the thick documents on the bookcase behind him.

"Thanks, man."

"No problem."

There was a pause as Amar watched Maxwell staring into space.

"You're still listening to that radio station," he finally stated. "Have you called her yet? It's been weeks."

Amar was the first person that Maxwell had met when he moved to Toronto nine years ago. They were both junior associates at the time and had become close friends over the years. A couple of weeks ago, Maxwell had told Amar about meeting Simone when explaining why he was listening to an online broadcast out of Atlanta.

"Not yet, but I will."

"Man, what's happened to your skills? I'm losing all respect for you. You better do something before she forgets all about you."

Maxwell laughed at the teasing, feeling better than he had in a long time.

On his computer, he went to the home page for the radio station and found the bio page for Moni S. At the bottom, it listed her e-mail address. It took him almost twenty minutes to compose something and hit the Send button. The message had a few simple sentences:

> Hello, Simone, I hope you are doing well. I listen to your show regularly. The music is great, but you are incredible. I miss you too. Please feel free to give me a call.

His cell phone number was under his full name, Maxwell Harper.

Her response came the next morning, but Maxwell was out of the office doing an inspection for most of the day. By the time he opened the message, it was almost six thirty in the evening. He was at home, and logged on to his computer to do a little work before relaxing for the evening.

> Hi, Maxwell Harper. Thank you for your note. I'm doing okay, but my Jamaican tan has almost faded. ☺ How are you? I will try to give you a call this evening. Bye, Simone.

Maxwell smiled with relief and anticipation, but also kicked himself for waiting so long.

He spent about fifteen minutes on the computer with work, then went into his bedroom to change out of his business clothes. July in Toronto was normally warm, but the city was now under a heat alert with the temperature near a sweltering ninety-five degrees Fahrenheit. Maxwell had been outside all day and eagerly stripped down to just a pair of sport shorts.

In the kitchen, he quickly seasoned a couple of steaks and chopped up a fresh zucchini from his garden. Then he went outside and spent a few minutes grilling his dinner. His house was in a popular part of Toronto called High Park, named after the large city park that extended down to the city's lakeshore. It was a neighborhood filled with older homes and mature lots. Maxwell had chosen it because the property sizes were more generous than most in the city. At the time he bought it, he had the vision of a lush garden that would be his own private tropical oasis.

While the barbecue heated up on the wooden deck, Maxwell stepped down to walk around his backyard and do some casual grooming. After his four years of living in the house, the landscaping was almost grown in. He had lined the fence with a variety of thick evergreens that created a tall privacy screen. Then there was a meandering row of five different fruit trees planted around a generous vegetable garden and a neat herb patch. All the produce was at various stages of maturity.

When his meal was cooked, Maxwell went back into the house to eat while watching the news and drinking a beer. Simone's call came at almost nine o'clock.

"Hi, can I speak to Maxwell please?" she asked when he answered.

The call display said it was a private caller, but he recognized her voice right away.

"Hi, Simone, how are you?" he asked politely.

"Hi, Maxwell. I'm good. How are you?"

"I'm all right. I'm glad you called."

She didn't say anything right away, so Maxwell plunged forward before he thought too much about what to say. "Listen, I'm really sorry for the way I left things between us. It was completely uncalled for and I wish I could take it all back."

"I'm sorry too, Maxwell," she replied. "I should

have been more direct with you after what your cousin told me. I just didn't know what to say."

"Don't be sorry. My behavior had nothing to do with you. I knew going to Cedric's wedding was going to be hard, but I guess I didn't realize how much it would affect me. But you didn't do anything wrong."

There was silence over the phone line.

"I knew the things she told me weren't true, Maxwell."

He laughed, trying to lighten the mood. "I'm sure some of them are true. I was a bit of a hot-head in my youth. There are lots of things I did that I'm not proud of, but messing with my cousin, April, wasn't one of them."

"Still, anyone who knows you can see that something like that just isn't in your nature," she insisted.

Maxwell had to smile at her fierce defense of his character. After years of having everyone believe the worst of him, her words tugged at the strings of his heart. "I'm not the same person I was when I left Atlanta nine years ago, Simone. Unfortunately, they don't know me at all now. That was my choice and for a long time I thought it was the right decision. But, after seeing Cedric again, I realized it was stubborn and cowardly."

"Why did you stay away so long?"

He let out a deep breath, surprised that he didn't mind discussing it with her. Other than the recent conversation with Cedric, Maxwell had not spoken to anyone else about these feelings.

"Lots of reasons, but mostly it was pride. We were living in Canada when my mom met Pop. He was from Atlanta, so we moved there after they got married. Cedric was born about a year later. So I always knew he wasn't my father. My real father was somewhere in Jamaica, but Mom never talked about him. Pop was the only father I ever knew. For years, I did everything I could to please him. But as Cedric and I grew older, it was pretty clear to me that he never considered me his son." He paused, trying to stick to just the basics for now. "Anyway, life with my step-father wasn't easy, but I didn't make it easy either."

"Oh, Maxwell, that sounds horrible," she whispered.

"Hey, I survived, and it wasn't really so bad. It just got to a point where it was better for everyone if I left, particularly my mom. She was always caught in the middle between us. I didn't want her to have to do that anymore."

"But she must miss you so much."

"I know. That's another one of my regrets," he admitted.

Neither of them spoke for several seconds.

"So, tell me about some of these exploits that you're not proud of," Simone said finally.

Maxwell heard the teasing in her tone and laughed deeply. "Okay, that's enough sharing for one day. I don't want to scare you off so soon."

"I don't scare easily, Maxwell."

He smiled, feeling like a giant weight had been lifted off his chest.

"What's going on in Toronto?" she asked.

Their conversation went on for over two hours. He spent time talking about where he lived and life in Canada, but they mostly shared their thoughts on a variety of topics. When it was time to go, they were both reluctant. Simone gave him her cell phone number.

"I really have missed you, Simone St. Claire. More than I thought possible."

"Do you wish we had stayed strangers?" she asked, referencing his final words to her in Jamaica.

"Of course not. My only regret was not spending that last night with you."

"Mine too."

"Can I call you tomorrow night?" he asked.

"I would like that."

They hung up soon after.

Maxwell went into his bedroom and opened his dresser drawer. He picked up the scrap of fabric that was neatly folded in the corner. It was the pair of panties he had removed from her body their last time together in the garden. He rubbed the delicate lace between his fingers before refolding it and putting it back.

Chapter 13

"I can't believe I'm twenty-eight years old and still single," groaned Maya.

"Well, that's the reality of life in Atlanta. There are too many attractive, successful black women, and too few comparable single men to go around. So either get happy single, learn to share, or go hunting in new woods," replied Natasha.

Simone and Maya burst out laughing.

It was Friday night, and the two girls were at Simone's apartment having drinks to celebrate Maya's birthday. Simone had made her famous cosmopolitan martinis and served a variety of pastries she had picked up from a local bakery. They were lounging in her living room listening to music and feeling slightly tipsy.

Maya had been looking at a framed picture of the three of them, taken almost five years earlier at their college graduation. She eventually put it back on the side table.

"Ain't that the truth!" Maya stated. "There's this new analyst in the firm. He's tall, well dressed, and pretty damn cute for a white boy. I know he's been flirting with me, but I've ignored him so far. Maybe I need to check out his woods!"

They all laughed again.

Maya was slightly shorter than Simone, with a sleek, slender frame. She had a light complexion with a brush of freckles across her cheeks. With her wavy brown hair, she often got mistaken for Spanish, and was constantly hit on by men of every culture.

Natasha was the shortest of the three and the darkest with skin the color of rich cocoa. Her frame was trim and athletic, and she wore her hair long and straight.

"What about you, Natasha?" Simone asked. "You're still single. What's your choice?"

"That's right. I'm single and loving it! I can do whatever I want with whomever I want, and he can bring a hot male friend along if he wants."

They laughed harder.

"So that's what you mean by sharing," declared Simone.

"Sounds good to me!" Maya chimed in.

"At least you don't have to worry, Simone. You have one of those elusive Atlanta men," stated Natasha when they had calmed down

"I've never worried," Simone replied. "Being single never bothered me."

"You've always been so lucky with men," Natasha told her.

Maya nodded in agreement.

"In what way?" questioned Simone

"You dated that football player for a couple of years in college. Then there was that dentist for almost a year. Now there's Kevin Johnson, retired boxer."

"You're right," Simone conceded. "I've gone out with some good guys, and I'm sure they will make great husbands for some other girl, but they just weren't the right one for me."

"God, Simone, you're so naive sometimes. All this talk about sparks and the right connection. This is the twenty-first century! That stuff doesn't exist anymore. I'm sorry, but the most a woman can hope for these days is compatibility, respect, and decent sex. And not necessarily in that order either. Anything else is extremely rare or just fantasy," Natasha lectured.

"Amen to that!" Maya chimed in.

"What if I told you that I've found that spark?" Simone told them with a secret smile.

They both just looked at her, not having a clue what she was talking about.

"What if I told you that I met a man that I fell in love with after three days, and that he did things to my body that made me scream and beg for more?"

"Simone St. Claire, you sneaky bitch!" Maya yelled.

"Who? When?" demanded Natasha.

Simone threw her head back and giggled wildly at their reactions.

"Come on! Stop playing," added Maya. "Spill it."

"Okay, here goes. His name is Maxwell Harper and I met him in Jamaica."

"Oh no! Not a Jamaican, Simone! Those men are the biggest playas out there! Look what happened to poor Terry!" Maya moaned.

"No, he's not a Jamaican. Well, he is Jamaican by birth but he's Canadian now," she clarified impatiently. "Anyway, I was hooked the first time I saw him. I mean, like heart-beating, body-singeing hooked. We got to spend three days together before Amy's wedding and I knew he was the one."

"Oh, Simone, that sounds so romantic," said Maya.

"It was."

"Simone, come on," Natasha said, clearly still shocked. "How can you fall in love in three days? And with a total stranger in another country? That's like meeting your true love on the Internet or something. You don't know anything about him!"

"Well, Natasha, killer of all joy and happiness, it turns out that Maxwell Harper is Amy's new brother-in-law!"

Simone didn't mention that she fell in love before she knew who he really was. She didn't need to add fuel to Natasha's perpetual negativity.

"What about Kevin?" Natasha persisted.

"Natasha!" Maya yelled. "Can you be happy for her? She's in love."

"I am happy for her, but I'm just saying she already had a boyfriend, that's all."

"Well, maybe she'll just date them both."

"Hello!" Simone interrupted. "I'm right here and I can tell you what I'm going to do. I will tell Kevin that we can't go out anymore, that's all. And, Natasha, he was never my boyfriend."

"Well, that's what he's been telling everyone," she countered.

"That doesn't make it so."

"Look, I wouldn't be a real friend if I wasn't honest with you. I think you're living in a fantasyland and you're making a big mistake," Natasha stated before she drank down the last of her cocktail.

Simone just smiled sweetly, used to her friend's negativity. To make matters worse, liquor always made her dour. Poor Maya just looked back and forth between them wishing that they could all just get along.

When Natasha and Maya finally left in a cab, it was just after midnight. Simone was still wide awake, so she poured herself the last of the sweet martini and lay on the couch watching television. She was feeling so good that nothing, not even Natasha, could ruin her mood.

She and Maxwell had been talking on the phone every day for over a week and a half. In the last conversation earlier that evening, he brought up the question of when they would see each other again. The big Caribbean festival in Toronto was a week away and he suggested she come and spend the weekend with him. Simone promised to think about it and let him know by Monday.

Simone was so excited she could barely contain herself. She was also a little scared of what all this would lead to, but was determined to live in the moment. The future would take care of itself.

Natasha was right about one thing. She did need to do something about Kevin. He had invited her out twice since their last date, but she had claimed she was busy. It was now time to be straight with him, and it had to be done before she saw Maxwell again.

They had spoken yesterday and he had invited her to the launch of a new high-end clothing line on Saturday. Simone decided it was the perfect opportunity for her to talk to him. She called him first thing in the morning and confirmed.

Once again, Kevin's brother, Donald, tagged along as well, but having him there worked in Simone's favor this time. It made it easier for her to wait until the end of the evening to talk to Kevin.

The event was being held in the ballroom of a hotel in downtown Atlanta. After the fashion, the crowd mingled around sipping cocktails and eating finger foods. They stayed at the after party for a couple of hours before Kevin was ready to leave. Simone went to the bathroom at that point, then spent several minutes trying to find Kevin again in the throng of people. When she did, he and Donald were in the back of the room near the rear exit. As she approached, it was clear they were having a very heated argument.

"Look, Kev, it's now or never, man. Once we accept this fight, you have to win. There will be too much riding on it!"

"I get it, Don!"

"Then get serious about your training! They're talking about a purse over ten million! We can't walk away from that kind of money."

They both stopped when they saw her appear out of the shadows. Donald nodded to her and walked away.

"You ready to go?" Kevin asked her.

"Yeah. Is everything okay? What's going on?"

"Nothing, just business," he replied casually as he guided her toward the front door.

Simone didn't press, but was surprised by what their heating discussion had implied. For the weeks she had known him, Kevin had spent hours almost every day training. He also followed a rigid diet and was always taking vitamins and drinking herbal teas. In the few times they had talked about boxing and his current business, he had never mentioned coming out of retirement, so Simone has assumed it was a routine for him.

When they reached the hotel entrance, there was a photographer in the lobby and he stopped them on their way out.

"Mr. Johnson, can we take a picture?"

Kevin pulled Simone close with a possessive arm around her waist. The camera bulb flashed with a series of shots. They left the event right after and headed to his car parked nearby. Donald followed them a few steps back.

"Kevin, there is something I need to talk to you about, privately," Simone said. "Can we go somewhere alone?"

"Okay, I'll tell Don to take a cab."

She sat in the passenger seat and watched the brothers talk again. They didn't appear to be as angry, but she could sense that their argument wasn't as unimportant as Kevin made it out to be.

There was very little conservation during the drive to Buckhead. Kevin took two phone calls, and Simone stared out the window. He stopped at a café not far from her apartment.

"So what's up?" he asked after they were seated at a table.

They had ordered two cups of cold sweet tea. Simone sipped hers, then plunged forward, choosing not to dance around the issue.

"Kevin, I've been doing a lot of thinking and I can't go out with you anymore."

He didn't respond right away, except to lean back and slouch lower in this chair. His eyes stayed fixed on her until she looked away first.

"I think you're a great guy, I really do, but I don't see us having a future."

"Why?"

It was a simple question, and Simone could not think of an easy answer. She chose to be honest. "We don't have anything in common. Your lifestyle is very busy because of who you are and your business. I understand that, but it's not the lifestyle I want."

"You've got to be kidding me!" He smirked. "So what? I'm too successful? You chicks don't know what the hell you want."

"Wait a minute," she interrupted, her own temper

flaring. "You're not talking to some chicks, you're talking to me, and I do know what I want."

"Whatever!" he replied, flicking his hand at her.

"Well, I guess that's everything there is to say."

"I knew I should have tapped that ass the first night. Now you think you're too good. You ain't nothing! Bitches like you are a dime a dozen."

"Good-bye, Kevin, and lose my number."

Simone grabbed her purse, stood up, and walked out the door.

Chapter 14

When Simone strolled into the station on Monday morning, she had a bounce in her step. She and Maxwell had spent hours on the phone talking about what they would do for the weekend in Toronto if Simone was able to go. He told her all the about Caribana, the largest Caribbean parade in North America, drawing over one million people every year. It was filled with music and dramatic costumes. Simone thought it sounded similar to Mardi Gras and was excited about attending.

They also contemplated other tourist sites nearby, like the CN Tower, or Niagara Falls. Maxwell assured her that he was open to whatever she wanted to do, or they could just hang out in his neighborhood. All she needed was to confirm the time off and he would take care of the rest, including the plane fare.

Before her show started, Simone secured a replacement for her time slot for both the coming Friday and the following Monday. She eagerly sent Maxwell a text message telling him she could be there as early as Thursday night. He responded immediately to say he would check out flights for her.

* * *

By Wednesday afternoon, Simone was giddy with excitement. She could not believe that tomorrow, at that time, she would be getting ready to go to the airport for a short flight to Canada and Maxwell would be waiting for her at the airport. As promised, he had taken care of everything, and an electronic ticket had been e-mailed to her last night.

She and Michael were walking out of the studio toward the parking lot when the station's receptionist, Cara, waved for her to come over. When Simone approached, Cara fluttered the pages of that day's newspaper, clearly excited about something in it.

"Hey, Cara. What's going on?" Simone asked her.

"Girl, no wonder you've been walking on clouds lately. Look at you looking all glamorous in the paper!" squealed Cara.

"What?" Simone said.

"Haven't you seen it? It's you with that hotty, Kevin Johnson. Right here. They even got your name right!"

"What?" she demanded, grabbing the page.

Michael heard the commotion and joined them.

"Oh my God!" Simone stated, unable to believe what she saw.

There she was, pressed tightly against Kevin's side by his possessive grip. The caption underneath said in bold black letters: ATLANTA BOXER KEVIN JOHNSON WITH HIS GIRLFRIEND, SIMONE ST. CLAIRE.

It was the picture taken last weekend after the fashion show. Then Simone saw the title at the top of the page: FORMER CRUISERWEIGHT CHAMPION RETURNS FROM RETIREMENT. FIGHT WITH EDDIE COSTILLO BOOKED FOR SEPTEMBER IN VEGAS. It was touted to be the most anticipated comeback in years. The rest of the story summarized Kevin's career and his title fight two years before. They also mentioned Donald, who was his manager, and his controversial promoter, Bob Bookman.

"Oh my God!" Simone repeated, feeling faint.

She ran out of the office with the newspaper still clutched in her hand. Michael and Cara stared after her as if they thought she was crazy. On the frantic drive home, all Simone could think about was Maxwell. What if he saw this picture? How would she explain it when she'd never even mentioned dating someone else?

"This can't be happening," she said out loud to herself.

In the time it took to reach her apartment, she managed to convince herself that it was probably just a local story. Kevin was an Atlanta native, so it made sense that they would make a big deal about his return to boxing. At the most, it would probably be limited to the United States. What were the chances that it would reach Canada? Or that Maxwell would actually read it?

Simone tried to take comfort in her logic, but something in the back of her mind told her it was wishful thinking. Boxing was big news everywhere, particularly when one of the most popular American boxers intended to return from retirement. There was a very real possibility that every major newspaper in the world had printed the story and the picture that went along with it.

Despite her trepidation, Simone called Maxwell at six o'clock that evening, around the same time she usually did. He didn't answer, so she left a message for him to call her back. She tried to sound happy and excited, but knew she probably came off as nervous and anxious. Then she sat on her sofa and waited for his callback.

Her cell phone rang three times, but none of the calls were from Maxwell. Simone ignored the two from Maya and particularly Natasha. The article had been printed in the sports section of the paper she worked for, so Simone was surprised and annoyed that her friend hadn't given her some advance notice. Granted, Natasha was a junior editor in the Living section, but she could have told Simone about it this morning.

The last call was from her mother.

"Hey, Mom," she answered. "You saw the article, didn't you?"

"Hi, baby. Your father just showed it to me. You looked beautiful, dear. The haircut really suits you. I wasn't sure at first, but now I can see how it complements your face. I was just telling your father that maybe I'll get mine cut too. We do have similar features."

Simone let her mother go on without interrupting until there was a pause.

"Thanks, Mom, but I can't believe they called me his girlfriend. Where did they even get my name?" she moaned.

"Oh, you know those reporters. They have people who research that stuff. You're a media figure too, dear, so I'm sure who you are is fairly common knowledge. I thought you were going to break up with that Kevin fellow?"

"I did. I told him that night that I couldn't see him anymore."

"Well, I wouldn't worry about it. You know how this stuff is. It passes and people just forget about it. It was a nice article, though. Your father was just telling me about the last fight Kevin had and how badly he was hurt even though he won. Such terrible violent business, boxing. I must say, I was not disappointed when you said he was not the right man for you. Not disappointed at all."

"Well, Mom, it's definitely over between us," she replied.

"What about your new friend? I hope he hasn't seen the pictures. He might not like the idea that you were dating both him and Kevin at the same time, dear."

Simone had finally told her parents about Maxwell several days ago, at the same time she told them she wouldn't be dating Kevin Johnson anymore. When they had asked how she met Maxwell, she revealed that he was Amy's new brother-in-law and they had met at the wedding, leaving out the other messy details.

"I don't know, Mom. I haven't spoken to him yet."

"Well, I'm sure he'll understand. Are you going to see him this weekend after all? You will really like Toronto. Your father and I spent a week there years ago. It's a beautiful city, particularly in the summer. It's hot, but not like in Atlanta. It's unbearable here and I can't wait to get away to the coast. You know, your father and I will be leaving on Sunday for Connecticut, so we won't see you for a few weeks."

"I know, Mom. I'm sure you guys will have a good time," she replied.

Somehow, her mom's incessant chatter made Simone feel better about the whole thing.

"Well, baby, I have to run. Your father said to tell you the show was very good today, but your contest is too easy. Kisses, baby, and we'll call you when we're back from the coast."

"Okay, Mom."

"Bye, my dear. And have fun with your new beau."

Simone smiled and hung up the phone.

Maybe her mom was right. Once she explained the situation to Maxwell, he would understand how irrelevant Kevin was. And even if he had not seen the picture, Simone resolved that she would tell him about Kevin anyway. It was a good thing they were going to be together over the weekend. There would be plenty of time to talk.

The phone rang again almost an hour later, while Simone was in her bedroom and still packing. She picked up the receiver, assuming it was Maxwell.

"Hey, girl," said Natasha to announce herself.

"Hey, Tash," Simone replied, trying not to reveal her disappointment in her voice. "I guess you're calling about the article."

"Yeah. You looked awesome, Moni. Those shoes were hot!"

"Thanks," she replied without interest.

"When did they take the picture?"

"After the Manny Brown fashion show last week," Simone told her.

"That's right. One of our reporters was there to cover the show," reasoned Natasha.

"Tash, why didn't you tell me the article was coming out? Didn't you know they were going to use that picture?"

"I didn't find out until this afternoon, Moni! I never get to see the full layout of the paper before it goes to print, just my section."

"Oh," Simone said, feeling her annoyance deflate.

"So, what's the problem anyway? Kevin has you on his arm while his return to boxing is announced. You should be excited."

"Yeah, except I told him we couldn't see each other anymore the same night the picture was taken."

There was silence on the other end of the phone.

"Wow, Simone. I still can't believe you're going to walk away from Kevin Johnson like that," Natasha finally stated.

Simone sat on the edge of her bed, frustrated by the repetitive inquisitions.

"Natasha, we've been over this so many times. Can't you just accept that he is not what I'm looking for? Why is that so hard to understand? I don't want to be with someone that doesn't stimulate me, that is not even interested in who I am. Kevin Johnson only wants a suitable girl on his arm, that's it. I need more than that."

"All right, all right," replied Natasha. "I get it, Simone. I just hope that you're not upset when you see another woman on his arm, that's all."

"I know you think I'm foolish and impractical, Tash, but I hope Kevin does find the right woman for him."

Simone heard her phone beep, indicating another caller.

"Natasha, I have to go."

"Okay. Are you still going to Toronto this weekend?"

"Yeah, I'm flying out tomorrow after the show."

"Okay. Have a great time."

"I will," Simone replied before she switched over to the other call.

Finally, it was Maxwell.

Chapter 15

Maxwell first saw the picture on Wednesday morning. He had gone into the office kitchen to get a cup of coffee, and caught a glimpse of it over the shoulder of a coworker who was reading the paper. At first, he was only mildly curious about Kevin Johnson, but noted that he stood beside a tall and very attractive woman. On the way out of the room, he took the discarded sports section back to his office.

It took a few seconds for his brain to register who the woman was, but the caption listing Simone St. Claire as the boxer's girlfriend ended any doubt.

Maxwell stared at the color picture for well over ten minutes, noting every detail of her image. Her beautiful face was made up to look glamorous and elegant, her expression serene. She wore a short, flowing black baby-doll dress that ended midthigh. The high-heeled black sandals on her feet made her curvy legs look a mile long. Maxwell's eyes always returned to the cocky grin on Kevin's face, and the possessive arm wrapped tight around Simone's waist.

The more he examined her picture, the more heated Maxwell got.

Simone St. Claire, *his* Simone, was Kevin Johnson's girlfriend. How could this be possible? Just two days ago he had bought her plane ticket to spend the long weekend with him.

Maxwell wanted to believe it was an old picture, taken long before he had met her in Jamaica. Then it wouldn't be so offensive, just a matter of history. But the simple piece of jewelry around her neck told him different. She boldly wore the amber necklace he had given her as though mocking him with her duplicity.

How on earth did Simone end up with Kevin Johnson, of all people? Though Kevin was a couple of years younger than he was, both he and Maxwell had grown up in the same humble neighborhood of College City outside Atlanta. Kevin's brother, Donald, had been in Cedric's class, and the three of them had hung out with him quite a bit during and after high school. He had left Atlanta around the time that Kevin was considering going professional after a very successful run as an amateur boxer.

Since then, Maxwell had followed Kevin's rise to the top of his profession, including the decision to make Donald his permanent manager. Maxwell was happy that the brothers stuck together as partners through the years.

Now, whenever Maxwell saw Kevin's arrogant posturing in front of the cameras, it was hard for him to remember the neighborhood kid he had been ten or fifteen years ago. Maxwell understood that the bluster and swagger were all part of boxing showmanship, but Kevin did not demonstrate any personality beyond that.

Maxwell finally folded up the sports section and

tossed it into the corner of his desk with disgust.
Why Kevin? Simone was so refined and sweet.
What could she possibly see in Kevin Johnson,
other than his flashy money and celebrity lifestyle?

He had to laugh at his own rationale since those
two things were usually more than enough to have
a lineup full of women waiting to be with you. But
not women like Simone, or so he had thought.
Now Maxwell had to wonder what he really knew
and didn't know about the woman he had fallen so
hard for.

The day dragged on for Maxwell. By five thirty, as
he made his way home on the subway, his thoughts
were swirling in his brain, and jealous anger sat in
the pit of his stomach. He was in the shower when
his phone rang, and he knew right away that it was
Simone. It was their routine to speak on the phone
almost every evening, usually around six o'clock.
Tonight, Maxwell stayed under the hot spray of the
water, not wanting to speak to her until he knew
what to say and how he was going to react.

When he did get to the phone, he noted the
missed call and that she had left a message. Maxwell
listened to her voice, as cheerful and enthusiastic as
usual, and wondered if it was all some big misunderstanding. Maybe she and Kevin were just friends and
the reporter just made an erroneous assumption.

Maxwell finally picked up the phone and called
the only person he knew that might have some
answers.

"Hey, Cedric, it's Maxwell," he announced when
his brother answered the phone.

"Maxwell? What's up, man?" Cedric responded,
clearly surprised. They had not spoken since the
day of the wedding.

"Nothing much. How was the honeymoon?"

"It was beautiful. We didn't want to come back!" replied Cedric with a light laugh. "How about you? How are you doing?"

The men spent a few minutes on short pleasantries before Maxwell got to the point of his call.

"Listen, Cedric, I have to ask you something. What do you know about Simone and Kevin Johnson?"

Maxwell heard Cedric's pause before he responded.

"I guess you saw the picture of them together," he finally replied. His sympathy was evident in his voice.

They had not discussed Simone in Jamaica beyond the intial explanation of how Maxwell had met her. Cedric's response made it clear that he now knew something about the relationship that had developed.

"Look, Amy told me that you guys had hooked up before the wedding. Didn't Simone mention Kevin Johnson?" continued Cedric.

Maxwell let out a long breath. "No. No, she didn't mention him at all."

"Wow," his brother said simply.

"How long have they been together?"

"I don't know, man. Amy mentioned a while back that they had gone out. Maybe a few weeks before the wedding. That's the last I heard."

"All right," said Maxwell.

"So, what's been going on between you two? From what Amy's said, I got the impression that you guys were still talking."

Maxwell let out a short, dry laugh.

"Yeah, something like that. She's supposed to be flying here tomorrow to stay for the weekend," he told Cedric.

"Look, Maxwell, I'm sure there's an explanation. Have you asked her about it yet?"

"Nah, she just called and left a message."

"Well, the only thing I can say is that Simone is as straight-up as they come. I can't see her playing those kinds of games. Amy's been trying to set her up for years, and it didn't matter what the guys did or how much money they made, Simone just said they weren't for her. One guy was a big-time investment banker, and there's another friend of mine that's a dentist. But she was never interested in any of that."

Maxwell just listened patiently. Everything in him said that was the Simone he got to know, but the picture of the sophisticated woman on the arm of a flashy pro athlete was hard to ignore.

"Well, we'll see," he uttered back to Cedric.

"What are you going to do?"

"I don't know, man."

"What exactly is going on between you two, anyway?" Cedric finally asked.

"Cedric, man, it's the craziest thing. We met and hung out for a few days. At first, I just intended to have some fun, and it would be a vacation thing. The next thing you know, I'm planning how I can keep seeing her. I've even been thinking about when I can visit her in Atlanta."

"You, come back to Atlanta? Damn, Max, that is serious!"

The brothers both laughed at the joke, welcoming the lessened tension.

"Just call her," Cedric finally said.

"Yeah, I will," stated Maxwell.

"Hey, isn't this the weekend of the Caribana parade?"

They talked for another few minutes before hanging up.

Maxwell went into the kitchen and made a quick meal. After eating, he went out to the backyard and spent a few minutes watering his garden. Two hours later, he had done a couple of loads of laundry and straightened up the house. There wasn't anything else he could do to put off calling Simone back. He sat on the couch and dialed her number.

Simone answered the phone after a few rings, and sounded as though she was being interrupted.

"Simone, it's Maxwell," he stated.

"Hey there," she replied in a voice that indicated there was a smile on her face. "How was your day?"

"All right."

"I was just finishing up my packing," she rushed on. "What's the weather supposed to be like this weekend? I don't want to bring too much but—"

"Simone," interrupted Maxwell. "I saw the picture of you with Kevin Johnson in the newspaper today."

"Oh no! I was afraid of that. I guess boxing is big news everywhere."

He knew she was trying to make light of the situation, but he couldn't even crack a smile. Instead, he waited quietly to hear her explanation.

"I'm sorry, Maxwell. I had no idea they were going to put me down as his girlfriend."

"Are you?"

"No! Of course not. We've gone out a few times but that's it. But I told him that I can't see him anymore."

"Really?" Maxwell replied in a tone steeped with sarcasm.

"Yes, really, Maxwell. I'm coming to see you tomorrow, remember? Why would I do that if I was Kevin's girlfriend?"

"I don't know, Simone. You've never even mentioned dating anyone else."

"I know. That's because I had no intention of seeing him again after I met you."

"So much for your intentions. When was that picture taken?"

Simone didn't respond right away. Maxwell stood up and started walking around the room, too agitated to sit still.

"Last week," she finally confessed. "But that was the night I told him we couldn't date anymore."

"Oh, come on, Simone. We got back from Jamaica over a month ago. Are you trying to tell me this was the only opportunity you had to stop seeing him? And then you had to go out with him to do it? Most people just break up over the phone."

"You don't believe me."

Simone said the words as though she was disappointed in him. As though he had let her down. Maxwell stopped pacing, confused by her reaction.

"Look, all I know is what I saw," he replied defensively.

"Maxwell, it was just a picture. You're right, I should have stopped seeing him weeks ago, but up until last week, I didn't think I would ever hear from you again. Then it seemed silly to break up with Kevin and sit at home hoping you would call me."

"How long were you dating him?"

She let out a long breath. "We met a couple of months before Amy's wedding. We only went out a few times."

"Do you have feelings for him?"

"Of course not! Maxwell, it was nothing, okay? He was just someone to go out with while I was single. I should have told you about him, I know that, but it didn't seem important. I mean, you've never mentioned any of the women you've dated."

"That's because they were all in the past. And

you're not going to find a picture of me hanging on to a rich celebrity like Johnson."

"What is that supposed to mean?" Simone demanded, clearly insulted by his insinuation.

Maxwell let out a long breath and pinched the bridge of his nose. He hadn't meant to say that. It just slipped out it the heat of the argument, and now he felt like an ass.

"Simone—"

"Maxwell," she continued, speaking over him. "I have apologized and I have explained what happened. It's obvious that you don't believe me, which means you don't trust me. But you have no right to insult me."

He let out another long breath.

"You're right," he told her simply. "And I apologize. That was uncalled for. I know we haven't known each other long and there are a lot of things we haven't talked about, but seeing you with Kevin Johnson just got to me. It reminded me of how little we really know about each other. You have a whole life in Atlanta that I don't know anything about. Everything has gone so fast between us that I forgot that."

"So, what do you want to do?"

"I don't know," Maxwell told her honestly.

He wanted to believe her, and really wanted to trust her, but Maxwell held back. For the whole day, he could not stop thinking that while he was hundreds of miles away missing her, Simone could be in someone else's arms. The image of her responding to Kevin the way she had with him made Maxwell's teeth clench with rage. He didn't want to feel those kinds of uncontrollable emotions.

"Do you still want me come and see you?"

"Of course I do," he replied without hesitation.

"Then maybe we don't have to figure it out now, Maxwell. It was easy when we were strangers, but if we want to be more than that, we have to spend the time it takes to learn the details. Do you know what I mean?"

"Yeah, I do."

"So, should I keep packing or what?" demanded Simone jokingly.

Maxwell laughed out loud and it felt really good. "Yeah, keep packing."

Chapter 16

Simone's flight landed at seven o'clock Thursday evening as scheduled. The process through customs went smoothly, and she had her luggage about twenty minutes later. The Pearson International Airport had dozens of flights landing every half hour, so the arrivals area was pretty busy. When she exited the secured area, there were even more people waiting to meet their friends and family, and no sign of Maxwell.

She paused for a moment, hoping that he would see her from wherever he was standing. Other passengers flowed around her to be greeted by those waiting for them, or toward the various transportation options. Simone tried not to panic as she finally started walking forward, unsure of where to head or what to do. Once she passed the crowd, she stopped at one of the benches near an exit door and parked her upright suitcase on its wheels. She then pulled her cell phone out of her purse, but there were no messages or missed calls.

Maxwell must just be running late, Simone told herself. She sat down to wait, making sure to keep an eye on the area in front of the customs exit so she would not miss him.

Though their conversation on Wednesday had started out rocky, Simone thought they had resolved the misunderstanding in the end. At first, she had been pretty upset about the way Maxwell had spoken to her, and it had really hurt to think he didn't trust her. But as he explained how he felt, Simone realized that he had every right to wonder what was going on.

She would have felt the same way if their roles were reversed. For example, when she had heard about the picture of Kevin with another woman at the benefit dinner, Simone had immediately assumed he was dating other people, and never even asked him about it. To be honest, she probably assumed the worst because it made it easier for her to trivialize anything that had been between her and Kevin, and relieved any guilt for what she was feeling for Maxwell. If she really cared for Kevin, she would have been heartbroken by the possible betrayal.

Before they ended their conversation the night before, Simone and Maxwell had reconfirmed her travel plans. Now that she sat waiting for almost ten minutes in the foreign airport, Simone wondered if she had underestimated how angry he had been. Maybe Maxwell changed his mind after thinking about it more. Maybe leaving her stranded in the Toronto airport was his way of getting back at her.

She shook her head to dismiss the idea, knowing deep down that he wasn't that type of person. If Maxwell changed his mind about her spending the weekend with him, he would have called and told her.

Simone checked her phone again, but there were still no missed calls or new messages. She was about to call him, but stood up instead, looking in every direction so that he would see her. Finally, there he was, walking toward her in smooth, confident strides from the opposite end of the terminal. He looked so good in his charcoal slacks and crisp white shirt, Simone wanted to run toward him, feeling overwhelmed with relief and excitement. Instead, she used the nervous energy to collect her things. When he was about eight feet away, she could not wait anymore and stepped forward to meet him.

They stopped in front of each other, and their eyes met to read each other's expressions.

"Hi," Simone finally said.

"Hi," he replied. "Were you waiting long? I went to get you something to drink but it took a lot longer than I expected."

"No, only about ten minutes or so."

They fell silent, eyes still locked. Finally, Maxwell's lips slid into an easy smile, and he pulled Simone into his arms for a deep hug. She let go of her suitcase so she could wrap her arms around him. He then pulled back and kissed her sweetly on the lips, followed by several soft pecks.

"I can't believe you're really here," he told her when they separated.

"Me either."

Maxwell kissed her again, this time with a touch of heat.

"How was your flight?" he asked as they started walking toward the parking lot.

He was pulling her luggage after handing her the chilled bottle of water.

"It was pretty good. A bit crazy getting to the airport, but otherwise okay," Simone told him.

"Are you hungry?"

"Starving, actually. They gave us the tiniest bag of pretzels, just to tease me."

"What do you feel like eating?"

"Hmm, I'm open. It's your city, so take me anywhere you would like."

"Okay, there are a few choices nearby."

Maxwell drove them a few miles from the airport, then escorted her into a casual and stylish restaurant. It was very busy inside, with a couple of large parties waiting for a table. Simone and Maxwell started with drinks at the bar but were seated within about fifteen minutes. Their waiter took their order and their meal arrived surprisingly quickly.

"Amy and Cedric sent you some of the pictures from the wedding," Simone told Maxwell while they were eating.

Up until then, they had been reminiscing about their time in Jamaica.

"Did they?" he replied with surprise.

"Yeah. I have them in my suitcase."

He nodded and continued eating. Simone took a sip of her white wine, and studied Maxwell's bent head. Eventually, he felt her gaze and looked back at her quizzically.

"Can I ask you something?" she requested. "What happened when you left your parents' home? I mean, where did you go? What did you do when you got to Toronto?"

She watched as he put down his fork and looked thoughtfully over her shoulder.

"I mean, you were what? Twenty-two? I just can't imagine moving to another country and never looking back. I moved out into my own place around that age, but my parents still live in Atlanta," she continued.

"Your situation is a lot different than mine was,

Simone," he replied in a mild voice. "I mostly felt relieved once I decided to go, and it seems extreme now, but just leaving the house wasn't enough. I didn't want to be in the same city. One of the guys I had gone to school with worked for a large company that had an office in Toronto. He sent my résumé in and they offered me a junior-level position."

"What did you do when you got here? Where did you live?"

Maxwell laughed a little at the memory. "Well, the timing wasn't perfect. It was early November, and I remember that the weather was colder than usual, somewhere around the freezing mark. I came about a week before I was supposed to start work and checked into one of those low-priced hotels. I had a little money saved, so I thought I would have about two weeks' worth of hotel money, plus enough for first and last on a modest apartment. What I hadn't factored in was how damn cold it was going to be, and how unsuitable my clothes were, particularly when we got the first snowfall of the year about three days later. So a chunk of money had to go to new clothes. Then I quickly found out that apartments in Toronto were incredibly expensive."

He paused to laugh some more. Simone smiled back, enjoying the story.

"Anyway, I was so broke that first month that I lived on tuna and rice. I must have lost about fifteen pounds."

"Did you miss anything about Atlanta, not even the weather?"

"Oh yeah! By February, I was ready to swallow my pride and go back. Then another snowstorm shut down the airports so I was stuck here."

Simone giggled.

"Did it take a long time to adjust to all the differences, like the weather?" she asked.

"Not really. After that first year, the winters weren't that bad. You know what it's like when you're young. You get involved in stuff and everything is an adventure."

"You make it sound like you're an old man!"

"Not old, but not twenty-two anymore, that's for sure," he teased. "Toronto isn't that much different from Atlanta in a lot of ways. We have access to all the same commercial things like music and other stuff. But then there are areas where the two countries are vastly different, like politically and socially."

They had finished eating, and their waiter brought the bill. Maxwell flatly refused her offer to contribute money.

"I told you, all you had to bring was your clothes. I will take care of everything else," he stated emphatically.

Simone yielded to his wishes.

When back in his car, they headed into the city through a series of highways. Simone looked out the car window at the cityscape around them. It was a few minutes after nine o'clock and the sun was starting to set. The darkening sky was illuminated by lights everywhere, from the streetlamps to the lights on hundreds of buildings and skyscrapers.

Maxwell spent the rest of the drive pointing out different landmarks and tourist sites. When they were turning off the highway closest to his house, he showed her the area on the lakeshore where the large Caribbean parade would take place on Saturday. He also pointed out High Park, a park that was almost four hundred acres, and included many attractions and facilities, including an outdoor theater, ballparks, gardens, restaurants, and a zoo. A large part of it was undeveloped.

They pulled into his driveway one block north of the park. Simone was surprised to see a charming Victorian house with a lot of the original architecture and details. She followed Maxwell to the front door, taking in the well-maintained front lawn and trimmed shrubs that lined the front porch.

The front foyer led right into a living room and dining room space with walls painted in a neutral tan. A wooden staircase ran along the right wall and led upstairs. The inside had clearly been renovated to create an open space on the main floor, but lots of the period trim and moldings were still there, painted in a soft white. There wasn't a lot of furniture, just a sofa and an entertainment unit in the living room, and a small table with four chairs in the dining room. There was also little decoration or artwork, but everything was neat and tidy.

"Maxwell, this is such a pretty house," Simone told him while still looking around. "It's not at all what I expected."

"What did you expect?" he asked.

"I guess I pictured you in a trendy loft or a sleek condo, or something. But now that I see you in here, this house definitely suits you. How old is it? A lot of the features look original."

"I don't know the exact date, but most of these houses date back to the late 1800s or early twentieth century. I think the floors and the staircase are original, but some of the other things were part of a large renovation. I was really impressed when I saw it. I was afraid that the remodeling would have removed all the details in the effort to modernize the house."

"It's really nice," she told him.

"Do you want to see the res

"Sure."

Maxwell put her suitcase near th
stairs, then started to show her the res
After the dining room, there was a sm
room and a coat closet. The kitchen was at
of the house, and it was very updated with
white cabinetry and dark brown granite counter
There were French doors that led to the backyard

Upstairs, there were two good-sized bedrooms, a
large bathroom, and the laundry room. He was
using one of the rooms as an office, and kept the
second as a guest room.

They then went up another flight of stairs to the
loft area that was his master bedroom. Like the rest
of the house, it only had the essentials. The area to
the right of the staircase had a large bed with a
simple dark wooden headboard, and a chest of
drawers. It was a large space and could easily accommodate a sitting area. Simone could not help
but imagine the wonderful potential.

The most unique feature was found when Maxwell
led her over to the other side of the staircase. Nestled
under a big window was a deep, oversized whirlpool
bathtub built up on a tile deck. The door to the private bathroom was to the right and had a sink, toilet,
and shower.

"Wow!" she said with her eyes fixed on the open
bath.

Maxwell laughed.

"Do you take a lot of baths?" she teased.

"Not really," he said, laughing harder. "But it
looks good."

"Well, maybe I can break it in for you while I'm
here."

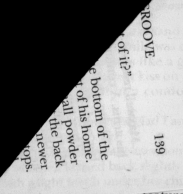

nd pulled her into
his lips.

"...eat idea," he told

...ss on ...r forehead.

...comfortable hug for an-

...at you're here?"

...Simone taunted.

...lifted her head

...is eyes searched

...her features as though memo-

rizing the details.

"Well, then I think I better show you," he declared.

His firm, contoured lips met hers and instantly ignited the smoldering fire that was always between them.

Chapter 17

Their reunion was not the romantic, sensual experience they had both imagined. Instead, it was hot, intense, and uncontrollable. That first kiss released the pent-up frustration they both had from weeks of aching celibacy and teasing memories.

Maxwell's mouth opened hers to taste and tangle with her tongue until she moaned with arousal. Simone's hands roamed over his back, remembering the hardness and strength. Then they were under his shirt, pulling it loose from his pants, and roaming over his smooth flesh. Her fingers urgently worked the front buttons to reveal his naked chest. She tugged at the cloth until it fell to the floor.

Her top hit the floor right after, and they were back in each other's arms kissing and stroking wherever they could find. Maxwell unbuttoned her jeans and tugged at them until they fell from her body. She stepped out of them and kicked them aside. He slowly removed his own pants, his eyes fixed on her standing in front of him in just a lacy pink bra and matching low-rise panties. Seconds later, he was naked and Simone now stared at his masculine perfection.

They came together again with labored breath and groans of urgency. Maxwell quickly removed her underwear, then ran his hand over her body, cupping and brushing every peak and valley. Simone bit at his neck and shoulder, loving the taste and smell of him. When his mouth found her nipple and his fingers brushed between her legs, she groaned loudly.

"Oh God, Maxwell."

"I've missed you so much," he told her in a rough voice between kisses and nibbles. "I can't stop dreaming about you at night."

He found the center of her arousal and rubbed it in small circles with his thumb. Simone responded with a low moan deep in her throat, and shivered from the sensations that coursed through her body. She sank her teeth into the skin above his collar, then bathed it with her tongue. Maxwell clasped her to him harder, his fingers delving deeper into her wetness. Simone bit him again. He sucked in his teeth and used both hands to grip her tapered waist and lift her off her feet. Her legs immediately wrapped around his hips while she held on to his shoulders. Maxwell steadied her with both hands under her bottom.

They paused in this new position for a few seconds, standing as one in front of the tiled bathroom, both still breathing hard with excitement. Simone was able to look down at him, and marveled at how incredibly feminine and delicate she felt held in his arms. His body felt so hard and powerful, yet gentle and sure. His eyes were dark and smoldering as they looked deeply into hers.

"Maxwell," she whispered.

That one word said everything about what she wanted.

Maxwell clasped her close and walked across the

loft to his bed. He placed one knee on the mattress, then gently laid her down. Simone released her arms from his shoulders and spread them out on the bed in a feline stretch, teasing him with a glorious display of her firm, round breasts. Her legs remained wrapped around him, keeping him close, loving the feel of his aroused shaft as it brushed the apex of her thighs. He leaned forward and ran his tongue down her stomach, dipping into her shallow belly button. She arched her back with pleasure.

When he pushed himself up on his arms, he looked up and down her torso.

"God, your body is beautiful. And these legs," he mumbled as he ran his hand over the back of her bent thighs, then down her firm calves.

Maxwell gently unwrapped her long limbs from around him, then stood up in front of the bed and brought her legs together so her feet faced the ceiling. Starting with her toes, he nibbled and kissed her skin, traveling his way down to the back of her knees. Then he gently spread her legs apart and worked his way back up until he was sucking on her toes.

Simone watched him with wide eyes, and shuddered at the feelings he evoked. When his hands trailed down the inside of her thighs, followed closely by his lips, she bit her lip in anticipation. Maxwell went to his knees on the floor in front of her, and continued his journey to the end of the path.

"Oh God," she muttered when his lips finally swept over her dewy mound.

Her moans and whimpers filled the room as he caressed her feminine folds with his lips, tongue, and fingers. Maxwell seemed to know exactly what her body craved, and he patiently satisfied her needs. Intense sensations flooded her, taking Simone closer and closer to the threshold of climax until she gripped the sheets beneath her with anticipation.

When she reached the crest, her body was gripped by wave after wave of sweet convulsions. The moment lasted so long that Simone thought she would collapse from the strength of it. She was completely spent when the last spasm rolled down to her toes. Maxwell planted several soothing kisses along her inner thigh, but she barely noticed. When he stood up and walked away, she missed his heat, but her bones were so flaccid that she could only turn her head to search for him.

He returned a few moments later wearing protection, lay down beside her, and pulled her into his arms.

"No one has ever made me feel the way you do, Maxwell," she declared in a soft, drowsy voice.

Maxwell sensed that she was talking about Kevin Johnson. He hugged her closer and kissed her temple, unsure of what to say. The taste of her arousal was still on his lips, reminding him of how she responded to him. Watching and feeling her orgasm had given him such satisfaction that he felt on top of the world, capable of moving mountains with his bare hands. In that moment, Maxwell did believe that only he held the magical key to her pleasure, and no other man could take his place. It was a primitive feeling, but filled him with masculine pride.

He felt the need to ask her more questions even though he wasn't sure he wanted the answers, but now was not the time. Now he wanted to hold her close, smell the scent of her skin, and sheathe himself deep inside her. There would be plenty of time to talk later.

It only took a few deep kisses for Simone's body to come alive again. When she was ready for him,

Maxwell inched his way into her wet warmth with gentle strokes. Simone wrapped her legs around him again, her hips thrusting to meet his and taking his length to the hilt. Maxwell shuddered at how good she felt, biting his lower lip and praying for control. They rolled onto their sides with their skin fused together. His thrusts started slow and measured but quickly became deep and urgent.

"God, Simone. I could stay inside you forever. I don't want this end."

Sweat broke out on their bodies as they undulated in rhythm, holding on to each other tightly. Simone came first with the soft waves of a second climax, and she cried out softly at the beauty of it. Maxwell watched her face and felt the hard throb of her body over his arousal. He was powerless to stop his own orgasm as it crashed down on him and left him breathless and out of control.

"Oh, baby . . . sweetheart . . . so beautiful!" he muttered almost incoherently, his words mingled with the last of her moans. ". . . love you . . . love everything . . . oh, baby!"

They feel asleep still wrapped in each other's arms. At some point, Maxwell pulled the sheet off one side of the bed and covered them with it. When he woke again, his mouth was dry with thirst and he was starving. He knew right away that it was sometime in the middle of the night. His alarm clock indicated the time was 1:16 a.m. Simone was still asleep, curled up with one of his pillows bunched under her arms. A drowsy smile played on his lips as he watched her.

It was still hard to believe she was here with him in Toronto. He was also surprised to feel the same intense and unrestrained attraction to her. There were many nights in the last few weeks when he convinced himself that his memory of her was faulty. He told himself his recollection was exaggerated and idealized. But now, as he resisted the urge to run a finger over the vulnerable curve of her cheek, he acknowledged that his feelings and reaction toward Simone were very real.

Where did they come from? Why could this woman occupy his thoughts and rouse his passion like no other? What was it about Simone St. Claire that had invaded his soul within days of meeting her? Yes, she was sexy, beautiful, and smart, but he had met many other women with similar characteristics, even dated a couple for long periods of time. None of those ex-girlfriends had ever torn those words out of his mouth at his most vulnerable moment.

"I love you."

He had said it, and meant it. It wasn't a flippant thing spouted during a breathtaking sexual moment. Maxwell had felt it in Jamaica, when his head told him to run but his desire had made him greedy to experience everything with her. But he had wanted to bring her here, to Toronto, to his home, and into the reality of his life. That was the only way he would know if this intangible, rare feeling was real.

It was.

So what happens now? he asked himself. Maxwell continued to watch her, smiling again when her deep breathing made soft whizzing sounds. There were no easy answers.

Finally, he left the bed and walked naked to the bathroom, turning off the lights in the bedroom along the way. Maxwell then went downstairs to the kitchen and grabbed a bottle of water. The growling in his stomach forced him to look in the pantry, and he ended up eating a large bowl of raisin bran.

Back in his bedroom, he tried to get back into bed without disturbing Simone, but by the time he got comfortable, her eyes were open.

"Hey," she said in a husky voice. "What time is it?"

"Hey," Maxwell replied while wrapping the sheet around them again. "About two o'clock in the morning. Sorry I woke you."

"It's okay. I didn't mean to fall asleep like that."

"Hmmm. Me either."

"Are you going to work tomorrow?"

"No, I took the day off."

"That's nice," she told him, rubbing his chest affectionately.

"So I'm all yours. What do you want to do?"

"I don't know. Maybe see a little of the city, do some shopping."

"Okay."

"Or we could just hang out. Go for a walk, see a movie. Do what we would do if we didn't live in different countries."

Maxwell sensed she was being humorous, but there was a sad truth to her words.

"Maxwell, I want to tell you about Kevin."

The words took him by surprise, and his spine stiffened immediately.

"What do you want to tell me?" he asked.

She let out a deep breath and took a moment to respond. "I just want you to know that there was never anything between him and me. We went out a few times, but we had nothing in common. Of course, my friends think I'm crazy, and insisted that I just needed to give it a chance. So I did for a while. But it was never anything more than that. I mean, we never got together or anything."

He knew what she was trying to say, but it was hard to believe it, no matter how he wanted to. Maxwell knew he had no right to care whether Simone had slept with Kevin or anyone else before they had met. But the Kevin Johnson he knew wasn't going to date a woman for weeks without getting something.

"Simone, it's really none of my business. I know I overreacted last night. I let my jealousy get the best of me and I'm sorry."

"Maxwell, I'm not telling you about Kevin because of the picture. We already talked about that. I'm trying to explain that I haven't been in a serious, intimate relationship for a while. For a long time, I wouldn't even go out with a guy if I didn't feel some kind of connection right away. I was completely okay with being single and just waiting for . . . something special.

"I know, it sounds juvenile. Trust me, I've heard it before. Anyway, meeting you in Jamaica took me by surprise. You were what I was looking for, but I could only have you for a few days."

Maxwell kissed her cheek, moved by her words.

"That's part of the reason I went out with Kevin a few times after I got back. I was starting to believe that I would never hear from you again, and I was a little angry that fate played such a cruel joke on me by taking you away. But it was pointless. Spending time with someone else only made things worse. All I wanted to do was be with you, even if it was only for a few days."

Maxwell held his tongue. He wanted to tell her that it wasn't enough for him, that it was too late for him to keep things casual or walk away. He was in this for as long as she wanted him. The other details about their lives just needed to be figured out.

But he had said enough tonight and didn't want to scare Simone. So he said nothing.

"So, what about you? Do you date a lot?" she finally asked.

Her voice was deep and throaty, as though she was falling asleep again.

"Sometimes, but nothing serious recently," he told her.

"What about girlfriends and relationships?"

"There have been a few. I dated one girl for almost two years, but we broke up over a year ago."

"Why?"

Maxwell shrugged. "Her name was Jennifer and things were fine between us. She was nice and we got along, but at some point she wanted more. I wasn't interested in moving in together or getting engaged, so we eventually went our separate ways."

He felt her look up at his face in the dark.

"Why?" she asked again.

Maxwell had asked himself the same question at the time. He was over thirty with a good career and doing okay financially. Why did he walk away from a good woman rather than move to the next stage of their relationship? He now knew the simple answer.

"Because I didn't love her."

Chapter 18

Their days together flew by with alarming speed. Maxwell took Simone for a walk through Bloor West Village to browse in the trendy boutiques. They then went over to Yorkville, Toronto's most upscale commercial area, for lunch and more shopping. She didn't buy a lot, but really enjoyed seeing a little of the city.

That evening, after dinner, they went for a walk down Yonge Street in the heart of downtown. It was after ten o'clock, and Simone was shocked at the volume of people hanging out within a six-block stretch near the famous Eaton Center shopping mall. They stood in groups watching people walk by dressed in the latest fashions, or drive up and down the street in souped-up sports cars, SUVs, and motorcycles. Most were young adults, probably between seventeen and twenty-five. It was like a large outdoor club without the music or the bar.

Maxwell explained that it was an annual tradition for the night before the Caribana parade. The crowd would loiter on the streets well into the night, meeting with friends or talking to whoever they were attracted to.

They stayed downtown for a couple of hours, strolling hand in hand and people-watching before taking a cab back to his house. Maxwell made love to her before they fell into an exhausted sleep. In the morning, they shared another round of passion in the shower while getting ready for the parade.

Caribana started at ten o'clock in the morning and they arrived just before eleven thirty. There were already hundreds of thousands of people lining the barricaded street. Simone and Maxwell found a comfortable spot on the grass near the end of the parade path. From there, they listened to lively music of the Caribbean played loudly by mas bands, and watched colorful floats go by, surrounded by revelers dressed in a dazzling array of themed costumes.

It was hot, over ninety degrees, but it didn't stop the crowd from enjoying the festivities and dancing for hours. By early afternoon, there were close to a million people shaking their hips to calypso, soca, reggae, and steel pans. Simone watched with surprise and amusement as young children and elderly people joined in the festivities. She even saw a few uniformed police officers get talked into dancing with the participants.

When they finally left the parade, there were still droves of people arriving, guaranteeing that number would hit close to 1.5 million visitors, and that the party would continue until well into the evening. They got back to the house before four o'clock and ate dinner at home. Maxwell barbecued steaks and Simone made a salad.

They rested for a few hours in the evening, cuddling together on the couch and watching whatever came on television. Maxwell then took her to a Caribana party on a large boat permanently harbored in Lake Ontario and converted into a restaurant. They danced for most of the night to R&B, soul, reggae, and calypso and occasionally relaxed on the upper deck in the night breeze and looking out at the city lights reflected over the lake.

It was after 3:00 a.m. when they got back home, and they could only strip down to their underwear before falling into an exhausted sleep. Sunday morning, Maxwell took her to a local grill for a late breakfast and they relaxed over coffee, eggs, and pancakes. This was their last full day together, and it was getting harder to ignore the separation that would happen on Monday afternoon.

They debated what to do with the rest of the day.

"How about I take you for a drive out of the city? We can go to Niagara Falls. Or up north and go horseback riding."

Simone's eyes lit up.

"I've never been on a horse before, have you?" she asked.

"Only a few times. One of the guys I work with goes regularly and bugged me until I went with him. It's easy. The horse does all the work."

"It sounds like fun, but to be honest, I would really love to just to relax," Simone told him.

"Okay, we can do that," he conceded. "Have you had fun so far?"

"It's been great! You have been an excellent travel guide once again. But I'm probably going to go back to work and need another few days off just to recuperate. My life in Atlanta isn't nearly this exciting."

"Seriously? I would have thought that as a media celebrity, you would be out at parties and things all the time," he told her.

"Maxwell, I'm hardly a media celebrity. GROOVE FM has a loyal following, but we don't exactly compete with the market leaders in Atlanta. My fame is very limited, trust me."

"So, what you do in your spare time?" he asked.

"I spend time with my parents or with my few close friends, like Amy. We go out every once in a while, but otherwise, we're pretty low-key. I also sometimes write for a local online magazine."

"Yeah? What do you write?"

"It's nothing, really. Occasionally, I will do an investigative piece, like the story behind the news. But I haven't worked on anything for a while."

"What was your last article about?" he inquired, clearly intrigued.

"It was about a kid that had gotten kicked out of junior high for having a gun. It wasn't big news, but what I found interesting was that he was apparently a really good kid prior to that, though he came from a rough area. So I interviewed him and his mom, then talked with his teachers, et cetera. It turned out that he was being pressured to join a gang by other kids in the neighborhood, and when he refused, one of them threatened to hurt his mom. So he felt a gun was the only way to protect her if they made good on the threat.

"Anyway, I found it troublesome that the system punishes these kids that are victims of a cycle that they didn't create and can't escape, but does nothing to fix the situation. It wasn't a unique story, we've heard it a million times, but I think it's worth reporting on so people can see the faces of these kids and hear the lack of choices they have sometimes. I didn't really propose any solutions. It's way too complicated to treat in a short editorial, but I just wanted to raise the issue."

Maxwell's lips spread into a deep smile, revealing his strong white teeth. His eyes sparkled.

"What?" she demanded, unsure of what he was reacting to.

"I thought you said you didn't have the determination to be a reporter? Then you're out there interviewing victims of gang violence and writing their history. Like I told you, Simone St. Claire, you're more adventurous than you think."

Simone blushed, remembering the conversation he referenced. That last article had been posted in the online magazine just a few days before she had left for Jamaica, and it was her third within four months. Maybe it was time to do another one.

"It looks like I am," she finally agreed.

He laughed and she giggled with him.

After breakfast, they walked back to the house. They sat down together. Maxwell had his back against the arm of the couch as he leisurely flipped through the various television sports programs. Simone was lying between his legs against his chest and was asleep within a few minutes. Though her nap only lasted about ninety minutes, she woke up feeling rested and refreshed.

"What time is it?" she asked while nestling snuggly against his shoulder.

He was so hard and warm, smelling like soap and masculine cologne.

"Three fifteen," he told her. "Did you have a good nap?"

His fingers played with the short hairs at the nape of her neck. He was watching the last minutes of a soccer match.

"Hmm. It was great. I'm not hurting you, am I?"

"Of course not."

"You make the perfect pillow. I could easily stay here all day," she told him.

"Feel free to use me any time you want."

Simone gave out a sharp laugh. "You may regret that offer. I can think of many uses for this strong body."

"Nah, I won't regret it. And don't be afraid to include indecent acts. I don't get offended easily."

"Nice," she purred with a catlike grin. "I will remember that."

"Nudity is not a problem either. Or nude and indecent, if that's what you're into. I don't judge."

She looked up at him with laughter.

"I'm just saying, I'm there for whatever you need," he continued, his expression still stoic as he continued to watch the game.

Simone lifted herself up until her mouth was right against his ear.

"Exactly how indecent are you talking about?" she whispered. "'Cause I can think of lots of possibilities."

She used the tip of her tongue to swirl over the contours of his ear. He shuddered lightly and she smiled at the reaction.

"Well, why don't you tell me what you have in mind?" Maxwell suggested.

His face still held only mild interest, but his voice had deepened a couple of levels.

Simone licked her lips, then gave a very graphic and detailed suggestion in a low, hushed tone. The temperature of the air around them shot up several degrees. She was hoping to shock him into reacting, but he didn't even blink.

"We have time for that now, or do you want to save it until later?" he asked.

"Oh, please!" Simone cried, slapping him playfully on the shoulder.

Maxwell finally turned to look at her with a big,

bright smile on his face. "Simone St. Claire. You have a very dirty mind! I like it."

She laughed sheepishly and buried her face in his shoulder. His whole body shook as he chuckled also.

"Now look what you've done," stated Maxwell after they had both sobered. "You've got me all excited and standing at attention."

"Oh, really! Well, what do you want *me* to do about it?"

Maxwell took her around the waist and rolled her effortlessly until she was lying across his lap and she was looking up at him.

"Well, you caused the problem with your kinky talk. It's only fair that you fix it," he teased.

Simone closed her eyes as he leaned forward and brushed his lips against hers.

"When you put it that way, it would be rude of me to refuse."

She gave him a sunny smile, really enjoying their teasing banter, but it faded when she saw the frown lines on his forehead. With an index finger, she tried to smooth them away. "What's wrong?"

Maxwell shook his head and kissed her again, this time hard and probing. His lips opened hers and his tongue brushed silkily against the roof of her mouth. Many seconds passed before he pulled back again. The frown was gone, but his eyes still looked dark with intensity.

"What?" she probed again.

"Simone, would you ever consider leaving Atlanta?"

Her breath caught in her throat and she stared at him, wide eyed with surprise.

"I don't know. I . . ." she stammered.

"Never mind. I was just curious."

"No! I mean no, it's a good question."

Maxwell shook his head. "It's okay. I shouldn't have asked you that. It's way too soon for those kinds of decisions."

"I've thought about it," Simone rushed to say, cutting him off. "I mean, let's be honest, Maxwell, if we have any future at all, one of us is going to relocate."

He looked at her intensely again, as though trying to read her thoughts.

"Is that what you want?" he asked. "For us to have a future?"

Simone didn't have to think about it. She knew the answer long before she had come to Toronto. She ran her hand up his shoulder and neck until she was cupping the back of his head. "Yes. Do you?"

"God, I can't even stand the thought of you leaving tomorrow!" he stated while his eyes remain fixed on hers. "Yes, I want a future with you, Simone. I want you here with me, in my home, in my bed, or anywhere else that will work."

She smiled up at him, filled with joy and excitement, but sad that their time together was almost over. Her throat became clogged but she swallowed hard and fought back the tears.

"Then we'll work it out, right?" she whispered to him.

Maxwell nodded, then kissed her again tenderly.

"We'll work it out," he confirmed. "But right now, I want to love you."

That's what he did, right there on the couch in the middle of the afternoon. They came together with a new level of intimacy and tenderness, and when they both reached the peak, it felt like their souls were connected.

Eventually, Simone and Maxwell showered and

walked to a nearby bistro for dinner. They lingered
for a while drinking wine and talking about their
lives. Simone told him about her friends Maya and
Natasha, describing their personalities and the dy-
namic between the three of them. She even talked
a little about how they had reacted to the whole
Kevin Johnson situation.

Maxwell told her a little about his friends in
Toronto, like Amar at work, and other guys he hung
out with regularly. It was an evening spent sharing
the type of everyday information they had not had
time for before. That night, they climbed into bed
and held each other tightly before reluctantly falling
asleep.

Monday inevitably came, as did the time for
Simone's departure. Maxwell drove her to the airport and stayed with her as she checked in. The
separation was difficult, but they both tried to stay
lighthearted. She promised to call him the minute
her flight landed, and he promised to start looking
at when he could visit her in Atlanta. They kissed
repeatedly until the last possible moment.

Simone sat in the boarding area feeling more
sad and lonely already. She tried to distract herself
by browsing the few shops nearby, and flipped
through a magazine she purchased. Finally, with
about five minutes to go before boarding, she decided to check her cell phone. It had been off for
the whole weekend, and the message center revealed two new messages.

One was from her mother on Friday just checking
in and letting her know they had reached Connecticut safely. The second was from Natasha on Sunday
morning. Her tone was so odd that Simone listened
to the message twice to try and understand it.

"Simone, it's me, Natasha. I need to talk to you.

Please call me as soon as you can! Please! I don't know who else to call."

There was a muffled sound, maybe a sob; then the call ended.

Simone hung up her phone, completely perplexed. Natasha was usually so solid and in control; it was very disturbing to hear her so distraught.

The fight attendant announced the boarding of Simone's flight. While lining up with the other passengers, Simone tried to call Natasha back, but it rang into her voice mail. She called her home number and the same thing happened.

Simone spent the next few hours of the flight remembering the incredible time with Maxwell, and fretting over what was going on at home.

Chapter 19

The next day, the body of a woman was found in her apartment by the cleaning lady. Simone found out about it on the evening news.

She was eating dinner in front of the television, and listened to the report with only mild interest at first. The woman had been found in her bathtub and had apparently died from a drug overdose. Her name was being withheld by the police until her family could be identified.

The footage at the scene started with a shot of the victim encased in a white body bag and being loaded into a Fulton County Medical Examiner vehicle. The shot then panned out to show the apartment building in the background. A chill went up Simone's spine as she recognized the front of Natasha's apartment complex.

Her thoughts immediately went to the odd message from Natasha. Simone had tried to call her two more times since she returned to Atlanta, but still could not reach her.

Simone put down her dinner plate and tried for the third time, but again there was no answer. She called Maya next.

"Hey, Simone," Maya said when she answered. "Are you back? How was the trip?"

"Yeah, I got back yesterday evening. It was really, really good," Simone told her briefly. "Maya, have you spoken to Natasha today?"

"No? Why, what's up?"

"When was the last time you spoke to her?"

"I saw her Saturday morning. We went to the gym together."

Simone let out a deep breath.

"Was she okay?" she asked Maya.

"She seemed okay. Why?"

"I'm sure it's nothing. She left me a message yesterday morning and I've been trying to call her back, but she's not answering. It's just that she sounded really upset, so I got a little worried."

"Oh," said Maya. "Well, I'm sure she'll call you back soon."

Simone sighed. It made sense, but she still could not shake the odd sensation of panic that had settled in her stomach. "Did you see the news a moment ago? They found a dead woman in an apartment in Natasha's building."

"What? Are you serious?" Maya replied. "When?"

"I just saw it. They think she died of an overdose."

"Wow. Natasha must be freaking out."

"Maya, I'm really worried about her. It's not like her to be so unreachable. And you should have heard her voice in the message she left. It was as though something really bad had happened."

There was a pause on the line before Maya responded. "What exactly did she say?"

"Not much," Simone replied. "Just that she needed to talk to me and I should call her right away."

"I'm sure she will call you soon. Don't worry. You

know Natasha. She is more than capable of taking care of herself."

"You're right, it's probably nothing," Simone agreed. "Well, let me know if you hear from her."

Maya promised and the girls hung up.

Simone could not stop thinking about it for the rest of the evening, and even mentioned the situation to Maxwell during their nightly conversation. Like Maya, he assured her that everything would be fine.

Natasha Morgan was confirmed dead in a very small article in Wednesday morning's newspaper. The medical examiner's report would confirm the cause of death, but it appeared to be an accidental overdose of acetaminophen pills.

The next week passed by in a blur for Simone. The funeral was held that Saturday in Natasha's hometown of Huntsville, Alabama. Maya and Simone drove there together, and spent the weekend with the hundreds of relatives that made up the extended family. Natasha's mom sobbed nonstop through the services, often with great bellows of anguish. Everyone else cried silently while shaking their heads with disbelief.

For Simone, it took several days for the shock to wear off. When it did, she was left confused and angry. The Natasha she knew would never have done something as stupid as take over twenty painkillers by accident. Nor would she have deliberately tried to her hurt herself or commit suicide. The whole thing just did not make any sense. There had to be more to it.

Then came the guilt. It was so obvious now that something had been going on in Natasha's life that she had not told Simone about. That bizarre voice-mail message was even more proof. But Simone had been too wrapped up in her own life to really pay attention to her friend. In those last couple of weeks, Simone had even avoided Natasha's calls, not wanting to hear her opinions about Maxwell and Kevin Johnson. Now she was dead.

Two weeks later, Simone was still trying to get back to her regular life. It was hard to wake up and go to work, but she did it. She and Maya talked a few times but Simone avoided other people as much as possible. Her parents called a couple of times from Connecticut, as did Amy, but Simone felt too numb to really interact with them. Kevin also called a few times, trying to apologize for his behavior that last night they saw each other.

The only person that Simone really wanted to talk to was Maxwell. Maybe it was because he had never met Natasha, but Simone was able to be honest with him about the very complicated friendship the two women had had since college. She talked about the harmless competition between them, the things that they had very different opinions about, and the jealousy she had felt when Natasha had gotten the job at the newspaper. Maxwell became the person she could go to and bare her soul without feeling judged or scrutinized.

He listened patiently every day, and gave her as much time and attention as she needed. It was obvious that he was very worried about her and they talked constantly about seeing each other again. Maxwell confirmed that he was planning the trip to Atlanta and just needed to confirm the dates.

It was Wednesday afternoon, over three weeks after Natasha's death, when Simone got a call on her cell phone from Scott Claus, a freelance reporter.

"Is this Simone St. Claire?" he asked.

She was still at the radio station, but had finished her show, and was sitting at an empty desk in the office finishing up some paperwork.

"Yes," she replied, distracted while writing out song logs.

"Simone, my name is Scott Claus. I've worked with Natasha Morgan in the past. I was very sad to hear about her unexpected death."

Simone froze with surprise. "We all were. How can I help you?"

"Well, I was working with Natasha on something before her . . . accident, and I wonder if you are available to meet with me about it."

"I don't know what you're talking about. What were you working on, and why would you want to talk to me about it?"

"To be honest, I don't know if you can help, but it's very important. I don't want to say too much over the phone. It's better if we meet. Do you have a few minutes this afternoon?"

Simone didn't know what to say. "Look, I'm sorry. Unless you can tell me exactly what's going on, I'm not interested."

"Ms. St. Claire, I promise you that this is very legitimate. I'm a freelance journalist, and I often do stories for the *Daily World*. That's where I met Natasha," he told her. "We can meet somewhere very public, and I promise I will only take a few minutes of your time."

Simone could not think of any valid objections, and she had to admit that her curiosity was piqued.

They agreed to meet in about thirty minutes at a casual restaurant a few blocks from the radio station. Before she left the office, Simone did some research on the Internet to confirm his identity. As he had stated, Scott Claus was a well-established journalist with a focus on current events. Simone was able to read two of his most recent articles, both printed in the *Daily World*. She also found a grainy black-and-white photo of him.

When she entered the restaurant, Simone recognized him immediately. He was waiting for her at the bar and straightened up when she approached. Like his picture, he had an angular face and curly brown hair, but his eyes were a surprising emerald green. He was also taller and younger than she had expected.

"Ms. St. Claire? I'm Scott Claus."

"I hope you haven't been waiting long," she told him as they shook hands.

"Not at all," he replied with an easy smile. "Let's get a table."

"Okay, I'm here," Simone stated once they were seated. "What is going on?"

"Like I said on the phone, Ms. St. Claire, I don't know if you can help me but it's worth a shot."

"It's Simone."

"Okay, Simone. I'll get right to the point. About a month ago, Natasha gave me something that she thought might be an illegal substance, but she didn't tell me where she got it. Do you know anything about it?"

"No, I don't know what you're talking about."

"Are you sure? Did she ever mention anything that she was concerned about? Maybe a new guy she was dating, or something?"

"No, nothing," Simone replied while shaking her head. "Why are you asking about this now? It's been a few weeks since Natasha's accident."

"I was out of town up until this weekend. And, to be quite honest, with everything that had happened,

I forgot about it. I had sent the tablet to a friend of mine at a lab. He called me with the results yesterday."

"What was it?"

Scott hesitated, looked at her speculatively. He then shook his head.

"I've told you as much as I can. Anything more can be dangerous," he told her very seriously.

"Dangerous! Wait a minute! Are you saying that Natasha was in trouble because of whatever she gave you?"

"I don't know, but this thing could be big, so I'm not taking any chances, Simone."

Now she looked at him hard and assessing.

"You don't think her overdose was accidental," she stated with certainty.

He looked back at her but didn't respond.

"How did you even know about me? Natasha certainly never mentioned your name," Simone continued.

"We were . . . close. She mentioned your name a few times. I found your cell phone number in the address book on her work computer."

"Close," she repeated simply; then her eyes fell on the gold wedding ring on his left hand.

Scott had the decency to look away.

"I don't think I know anything that can help you, Scott. But if you think that this mess had anything to do with Natasha's death, you better get to the truth."

"That's what I intend to do."

Simone nodded, satisfied with his words and the sincerity on his face.

"Here is my card," he said while handing it to her. "If you think of anything else that may be helpful, please call me."

"Okay," she promised.

She was about to push her chair back and say good-bye.

"One more question," Scott said. "Did Natasha have any issues with Kevin Johnson?"

Chapter 20

"What do you mean? What does Kevin have to do with any of this?"

"I don't know," he told her. "I'm just trying to find a direction to go in."

"Well, Natasha never met Kevin."

"Are you sure?"

Simone let out a short laugh. "Right now I'm not sure of anything. Clearly, there were a lot of things going on in Natasha's life that she didn't tell me about."

"Natasha could be very private at times. Don't take it personally."

She looked away, feeling sad about the whole thing.

"Even if she knew Kevin, what could he have to do with all this?" she continued after a few moments.

"I'm sure it's nothing," Scott told her dismissively. "Like I said, if you can think of anything that might be helpful, call me."

He stood up and she did the same.

"It was nice meeting you finally, Simone St. Claire," he stated.

"You too, Scott. Good luck, and I really hope you find whatever information you are looking for."

They shook hands and he left the restaurant.

Simone stayed for a couple of minutes, thinking about Natasha and all the things Scott had told her. She also thought back to that ominous message left while she was in Toronto. What had made Natasha so scared and what did she need to tell Simone that Sunday morning? It could not be a coincidence that she apparently swallowed a handful of pills twenty-four hours later. Every instinct in Simone's body told her all these things were intertwined.

When she did leave the restaurant, Simone called Maya and they agreed to meet at Maya's house in Decatur at six o'clock. Simone had about forty-five minutes to waste, so she stopped at a grocery store along the way and bought some chicken and vegetables for dinner, and a few other items that she needed at home.

It had been several days since the friends had talked, so they spent the first hour or so getting caught up while they cooked dinner. They were sitting at Maya's kitchen table eating when Simone brought up Natasha.

"Did Natasha ever mention someone named Scott Claus to you?"

Maya thought for a moment, before shaking her head. "No, I don't think so. Why?"

"He's a reporter that works for the *Daily World*. I think they had some kind of a relationship, but he's married."

"Really? How do you know this?"

"He called me today to ask me about a story they had been working on before she died. When I asked him how he knew Natasha, he said they were close. The way he said it made it obvious what he meant."

"Wow."

"I know! I mean, why wouldn't she tell us something like that? Now I'm wondering what other secrets she'd kept from us," she told Maya.

"What do you mean?"

"Well, I thought the three of us were really close, and that we shared almost everything. But now I don't know."

Maya was silent for a few seconds. She put down her fork before responding. "Simone, how would you have reacted if Natasha had told you about an affair with a married man?"

Simone shrugged. "I don't know. I probably would have told her it was a bad idea and that she would end up hurt."

"So maybe that's why she didn't say something. You have to admit, Natasha wasn't like you. She wasn't always looking for something meaningful and long-term. Sometimes she just wanted to have a good time or live in the moment."

"Okay, but that's still no reason not to tell me. We were friends. I would have understood in the end."

The look on Maya's face said she didn't necessarily agree.

"What?" Simone insisted. "I'm not that judgmental, am I?"

"No, Simone, not judgmental. You're just a little idealistic when it comes to relationships, and Natasha was very practical, that's all. Neither of you was wrong or right, just different."

Simone didn't know what to say, but she felt like crying. Maybe she was too single-minded in her way of seeing things. If Natasha had felt more comfortable, maybe she would have told Simone about whatever was wrong in the end. Maybe Simone could have done something to prevent her death.

"I'm sorry if I ever made you guys feel like you couldn't be honest with me. I was so proud of Natasha's ability to go after what she wants. Even a little jealous, to tell you the truth," she confessed to Maya. "Anyway, this guy Scott says Natasha gave him some evidence and he wanted to know if I knew anything about it."

"What evidence?"

"He didn't want to say. Did she ever tell you about anything like that?"

"No, I don't think so."

"What about any new boyfriends? Or other friends that we didn't know?"

Maya looked away and bit her bottom lip.

"What?" Simone demanded. "What's wrong?"

"Simone, Natasha met someone about two months ago."

"Really? What did she tell you about him? 'Cause that's around the time that Scott says she approached him about this evidence."

"It was Kevin, Simone."

The words didn't make sense to her at first, even though Maya's face looked guilty and apologetic.

"Kevin who? Kevin Johnson? What do you mean?"

"Look, Simone, I'm sure Natasha only went out with him because you made it clear that you weren't interested. She would never have done anything to hurt you."

"Natasha went out with Kevin? When? How many times?"

"They met while you were in Jamaica. Apparently, he flirted with her pretty heavily at some club and gave her his number. She thought it was funny at first, but when you told her you were going to break up with him, she called him."

"This is unbelievable, Maya."

"I know, I know. I told her it was a really bad idea," Maya insisted. "She didn't tell me much, but I know she went to his place two or three times."

Simone just looked off into space, her mind racing with the information.

"Simone, she was supposed to see him again that Saturday. You know, before she did what she did."

"She should have just told me, Maya."

"I know, and she planned to. I told her that if she didn't, I would. Then after her . . . accident, it just didn't seem important. I thought it would only tarnish your memory of her. I'm so sorry, Simone."

"I am too," she replied with a deep sigh.

It really bothered Simone that Natasha didn't trust her, and didn't feel comfortable confiding in her, even if it was something that they might fight about. And now it was too late for Simone to fix it.

"Do you think Kevin has anything to do with what this Scott guy is investigating?" Maya finally asked.

"I don't know, but I'm definitely going to find out."

The two women spent another couple of hours talking. Simone caught her up on things with Maxwell, and that he was planning to return to Atlanta for the first time in over nine years to see her. Maya confessed that she was now hunting in a new forest. She had finally accepted an invitation to go see a movie with the new intern she had been flirting with for weeks and she was really excited about it. When she finally left, Simone felt closer to Maya than she had in a long time. She was still hurt and disappointed about the secrets that she kept but glad that everything was out in the open. With Natasha gone from them, girlish feelings of betrayal and duplicity didn't seem important.

Simone called Scott Claus first thing Thursday morning and arranged to meet him later that afternoon at the same restaurant. They got a table again, but this time also ordered drinks and appetizers.

"Okay, so what do you have for me?" Scott finally asked.

"It may be nothing, so before I tell you anything, I want to know exactly what it is that Natasha gave you."

"Simone, I told you, I don't know how big this thing is. The less you know the better, trust me."

"Well, it's a little late for that. You contacted me, remember? And now I'm involved and I think I need to understand exactly what I am involved in."

Scott let out a deep breath and sat back in his chair. She continued to stare him down until he looked away.

"Okay. She gave me a pill that looked like some sort of drug, maybe vitamins or an herbal supplement. The lab results revealed that it was a new form of anabolic steroids. Technically speaking, it's not illegal because there is no record of this particular combination of testosterone enhancers being used before. But if it is being used in professional sports, then it's big news. If you haven't been reading the sports news in recent years, there has been a lot of controversy and investigations into steroid use in baseball, wrestling, cycling, and other sports.

"So the capsule in and of itself has no real value. The real story is who is using it."

Simone's heart started beating like a drum. She had to force herself to say the words that were screaming in her mind. "Why did you ask me about Kevin Johnson?"

Scott shrugged. "My first reaction was that it was something that an athlete would use. There are lots of athletes in Atlanta, but I couldn't find any that had a connection to Natasha other than Kevin Johnson through you. So it was a hunch."

"Your hunch may be right. I found out last night that Natasha and Kevin were seeing each other for a few weeks before she died."

"Whoa! I thought you were his girlfriend. Are you sure? Natasha wouldn't do something like that to a friend."

"It's complicated. Kevin and I just went out a few times, that's all. I had made it clear to her that I was in love with someone else and I stopped dating Kevin. I know she would have told me about it sooner or later."

"Okay," he said, sounding very skeptical. "So you think Kevin is the one using the steroids?"

"I don't know. I think he was training really hard for his return to boxing. But don't steroids cause you to get really big and bulky? Or violent and short-tempered? I didn't really see that."

"Not necessarily. It depends on the dosage and how it's taken. Maybe he just needed an edge for training. Anyway, there's only one way to find out if it's him."

Simone didn't immediately see the direction he was heading.

"How?" she asked.

"We need to see if he's taking the same pills that Natasha gave to me."

"How are we going to do that? I can't exactly ask him. We're not seeing each other anymore anyway. I haven't even talked to him for over a month."

"Well, unless you can find the supply on him or in his place, we're dead in the water."

"There must be another way. Can't we just go to the police and tell them what we know?"

"Simone, we have no proof of anything. Certainly

not enough to force Kevin to take a drug test. The police wouldn't touch this with a ten-foot pole. No, we have to be certain before we go to the police," he insisted. "Look, I'm not suggesting that you do anything dangerous or offensive. You just need to confirm if he is the one using the supplements, that's all."

She let out a deep breath. "What happens if he is?"

He shrugged. "I'll write my story and hand over the evidence to the Georgia Athletic and Entertainment Commission."

"What will happen to him?"

"I don't know," Scott told her. "Doping hasn't been a big issue in boxing, but there is growing concern. He may just lose his license. But his comeback fight is slated to be the match of the year, and millions of dollars are at stake. Not to mention the money that could be made for pay-per-view. They could decide to prosecute him further."

"I don't know, Scott. I don't want to responsible for destroying his career or anything."

Scott reached out and took her hand. "Simone, you're not seeing the full picture here. Did Natasha seem like the type of person to take so many Tylenol pills that she overdosed? Of course not! I don't think it was just a coincidence that she ends up dead within a week of giving me that damn pill!"

Chapter 21

Simone didn't want to go home right away, so she went to the mall and pretended to shop.

The conversation with Scott had given her so much to think about that she felt restless and anxious. They had spent a couple of hours talking about what she needed to do, and formulating a plan. He showed her a picture of the capsule given to him, and also made it clear that neither of them should talk to anyone else about the situation until they had the proof they were looking for. By the time they parted, she agreed to try and see Kevin sometime before Monday.

Now she was second-guessing that decision. What had she gotten herself into? How could she go out with Kevin again, pretend to want to be with him, only to try and find evidence that could end his career? He was the darling of Atlanta. A success story of a local black athlete. What good could come of exposing his use of steroids, if in fact that was what he was doing?

Only one thought seemed to speak louder than her multiple doubts and objections. Kevin could be responsible for Natasha's death.

Scott Claus definitely believed that the steroid sample he had been given was connected to her overdose. He had no evidence, but Simone saw the conviction in his eyes. Yes, he could end up with a very big story to sell, but he also hoped for justice for Natasha. Now that was the only factor in all of this that motivated Simone to be involved.

When she finally did go home, it was almost nine thirty that evening. Maxwell had left a couple of messages for her on her cell phone, so she called him back as soon as she got in the door.

"Hey, is everything okay? I was getting a little worried about you," he said.

"I'm okay. I had a couple of errands to run after work," Simone told him.

"How was your day?"

"It was all right. How about you?"

"Not bad. Are you sure you're okay? You sound a little stressed out."

Simone could hear the concern in her voice and she felt tears well up in her eyes. *I would be so good to talk to someone about the situation, and have them help her figure out what to do.*

"Maxwell, I need to tell you about something."

Despite her promise to Scott, Simone told Maxwell almost everything. She held back about the allegation that Natasha's death might be connected. Simone knew there was no way he would tolerate her involvement if there was a possibility of physical danger.

"Stay out of it, Simone. This sounds like bad news," Maxwell eventually told her.

His tone was deep with alarm and inflexibility.

"Maxwell, it's too late. I'm already involved. At this point, I'm the only one that can get close enough to Kevin to find out the truth."

"No, it's out of the question! Think about the situation you will put yourself in. What if he catches you taking the pills?"

That was exactly what Simone was afraid of also, but she wasn't about to admit it to Maxwell.

"I'll just play innocent, pretend I thought they were multivitamins or something. I don't know," she improvised. "Maxwell, he doesn't even know that Natasha and I were friends. He would have no reason to suspect anything else."

She could hear his heavy breathing through the phone.

"I don't like it, Simone. This Scott guy is using you for his own gain and I think it's a really bad idea. Just stay out of it. Please."

Simone bit her lip, hating to hear him ask her for something that she couldn't give.

"I've already given my word, Maxwell. I can't just walk away now," she explained. "It's really not that big a deal. Kevin's called me a few times recently, trying to apologize for the way he acted the last time I saw him. So I'll just return his call and pretend I want to be friends. It's simple."

"I don't want you anywhere near that guy!" he barked. "I know I sound like a jealous ass, but I don't give a damn, Simone."

"Is that what this is about? You still think there is something between him and me? You still don't trust me?" she demanded.

"I do trust you, I just don't trust him. And I definitely don't want you to put yourself in a situation where he thinks you want to be with him. Is that so unreasonable?"

"Maxwell, if you really trust me, then you would know that I am doing what I think is best. I'm sorry, I know how you feel, but I have to do this."

He was silent on the other end of the phone, but Simone could feel his frustration.

"You're a grown woman," he finally stated. "Obviously, I can't tell you what to do."

"Maxwell, please understand," she begged.

"I understand, Simone. I just don't like it."

"Maxwell—"

"I better go," he told her, then hung up.

Simone put down her phone, though she wanted to throw it across the room. Her next instinct was to call him back, but what good would it do? Had she really expected Maxwell to be okay with the idea of her going out with Kevin again, even though it was just to investigate a story?

I should never have told him, she thought to herself.

Maxwell sat on the edge of his bed, also wishing she had not told him of this crazy, dangerous stunt she was about to do. His heart was pounding and his hands felt sweaty. All he could think about was stopping her.

But how? She still seemed pretty determined and he was a thousand miles away.

The next morning, after tossing and turning all night, Maxwell had made a decision. He was going to Atlanta as soon as possible. If he couldn't prevent Simone from participating in this fiasco, he could at least be there to make sure she did not get hurt. Once his mind was made up, Maxwell got busy making the arrangements. He packed a weekend bag and drove to the office. By noon, he had a ticket on the first available flight that afternoon, and arranged to have Monday off as a personal day.

Maxwell intended to call Simone as soon as her radio show ended and let her know to expect him, but he didn't get a chance. He ended up so rushed to wrap up everything at work that he barely made it to the airport on time.

His flight landed in Atlanta at seven thirty, and it was almost eight o'clock before he was able to catch a cab to Buckhead. He tried to call her several times during the ride, but she did not answer her home or cell phone. Finally, Maxwell called his brother's house. Amy answered the phone.

"Hi, Amy, how are you?"

"Maxwell, is that you? I'm good, how are you?" she replied.

"I'm good. Is Cedric around?"

"Yeah, he's just in the basement. I'll get him for you."

"Wait. Before you go, have you spoken to Simone today?" he asked, trying to keep his tone very casual.

"Not today, no. Why, what's wrong?"

"Nothing. Everything is fine. I've just landed in the city to surprise her, but she's not answering her phone."

"What? You're here? In Atlanta? That's great, Maxwell! Cedric is not going to believe this. One sec!"

Amy put down the phone before he could say anything else. He could hear her yelling in the background.

"Cedric! Cedric! Come up here! Maxwell's on the phone. He's here in Atlanta. Hurry up!"

Maxwell couldn't help but smile to himself. He hadn't really stopped to think about it earlier, but this was a pretty big occasion. There were a lot of people in the city who were going to be shocked.

"Maxwell, are you really in the ATL? Damn, bro!

That's great!" Cedric yelled into the phone while laughing.

Maxwell couldn't help but chuckle also. "Yeah, I'm here. I just landed a little while ago."

"So, where are you now?"

"I'm on the highway heading up to Buckhead. But here's the thing. I didn't tell Simone I was coming for the weekend. It was supposed to be a surprise. And now I can't reach her."

Cedric laughed harder at him.

"Yeah, I know. It didn't exactly work out the way I planned," Maxwell added dryly.

"Why don't you come by our place until you reach her? We're only a few minutes away from her apartment. I'll drive you over there when she gets home."

"Okay," Maxwell agreed.

He took the directions from Cedric and relayed them to the cabdriver.

The car stopped in front of a cozy bungalow on a mature street about fifteen minutes later. Amy and Cedric were waiting on the front porch, and welcomed him into their home with hugs and laughter.

"So, you really didn't tell Simone you were coming?" Amy asked.

They were sitting in the living room. Cedric handed Maxwell a beer and opened one for himself.

"Nope," he replied.

"She's going to freak out!" she added.

"That's if she ever calls me back," Maxwell stated sarcastically. "We had a bit of a fight last night. I'm not even sure she's talking to me right now."

"How long are you staying?" asked Cedric.

"My return flight is on Monday."

"Well, you're welcome to stay here."

"Cedric!" Amy admonished with a light slap on his

arm. "Maxwell didn't come all this way to hang out with you, no offense. I'm sure Simone will forget all about the argument when she sees you, Maxwell."

Maxwell smiled slightly. It wasn't their fight that had him worried about why he couldn't reach Simone, but he wasn't going to say anything to his brother and sister-in-law. He didn't know if Simone had confided in Amy about the situation with the reporter and the mystery steroids. There was no need for more innocent people to get involved.

"So, how is married life so far?" he asked, effectively changing the subject.

The newlyweds looked at each other, grinning like high school kids.

"It's all right," replied Cedric with an indifferent shrug, but his eyes remained stuck on Amy.

Maxwell looked back and forth between them. It felt so good to see his baby brother happily married and so in love with his new bride. Seeing them together now, in their welcoming home, almost made up for all those years they weren't in touch. Almost.

"Have you told Mom you were here yet?" Cedric finally asked.

"Not yet. I was going to call her tomorrow morning. It's a little late now," explained Maxwell.

"Hey, why don't we invite her over for lunch tomorrow? Then you and Simone can come over and spend the whole afternoon with us," Amy suggested.

"That's perfect. Dad usually spends Saturday afternoon at the track anyway," added Cedric.

Maxwell was about to respond when his cell phone rang.

"It's Simone," he told the others, then got up and walked a few steps away to answer it with some privacy.

"Hey there."

"Hi, Maxwell. Sorry I couldn't call you earlier," she said right away.

He closed his eyes tight and bowed his head. It was so good to hear her voice. He didn't want to acknowledge it, but when she didn't answer the phone earlier, he couldn't help but wonder if she had met up with Kevin and something had gone wrong.

"That's okay," he told her. "Where are you?"

"I just got home."

"Okay. Can I give you a call back in about ten minutes?" Maxwell asked.

"Sure."

"Give me ten minutes."

They hung up and Maxwell told Amy and Cedric that Simone was now at home. Cedric drove him to Simone's building, and fifteen minutes later, he was standing in her front lobby.

Chapter 22

Simone had just removed her dress when the phone rang the second time. It was Maxwell calling back.

"I'm sorry about last night, Maxwell," she said once they had greeted each other.

"I am too, Simone. I didn't mean to suggest that I don't trust you."

"I know."

"This is what makes a long-distance relationship so difficult. Right now we could be having makeup sex."

Simone smiled.

"We could try makeup phone sex," she suggested teasingly.

"Nah, it's not the same. Right now only the real thing will do."

"Well, you'll just have to take a rain check."

"I guess so," he told her, sounding like a little boy who couldn't have dessert.

The doorbell rang at that moment. Simone glanced at the clock on her nightstand, wondering who it could be at almost eleven o'clock at night.

"Maxwell, one sec, okay? There's someone at the door."

"Are you expecting someone?" he asked.

"No," she replied briefly.

Simone was only wearing her bra and panties, so she put the phone down on the bed and grabbed her robe from the back of the bedroom door. She then took the phone with her to the front hall.

"Who is it?" she asked loudly before checking the peephole.

"Cedric," was the reply in a muffled voice.

"Cedric?" Simone repeated with surprise. "Maxwell's brother?"

She could see the back of his head. Worried that something was wrong, Simone tied up her robe and rushed to unlock her door.

"Is everything okay?" she asked as soon as she stood before him.

"Everything is fine," he responded, then turned to face her.

Except it wasn't Cedric at all. It was Maxwell standing before her, looking tall and masculine, and with a tote bag over his shoulder.

Simone was frozen with shock and disbelief. He still had his cell phone pressed to his ear, but then hung it up and slipped it into his pants pocket.

"Oh my God! Maxwell? What—"

"Surprise!" he said with a big grin on his face, clearly enjoying the moment.

He stepping over her threshold and took her into his arms. Simone immediately buried her face into his shoulder and pulled him closer. She was so overwhelmed from the touch and smell of him that her body started to tremble from the rush of emotion.

"Maxell," she said simply.

Her voice faltered and he pressed a kiss on the

top of her head. They stood like this for over a minute. Finally, Maxwell guided them a couple of steps inside and closed the apartment door. He took her phone, still clenched in her hand, and put it down on the small console table along the wall. Simone looked up into his eyes. Her own were shiny and glowing with unshed tears.

"I can't believe this! When did you get here?"

"A couple of hours ago," he told her gently.

"Why didn't you tell me you were coming? I would have met you at the airport."

"I know. But then it wouldn't have been a surprise, right?"

"How long can you stay?"

"Until Monday," he stated, clearly distracted as he looked down between them to examine her body wrapped in a gray satin robe. "Wow. I've spent all day imagining this moment, but reality is so much better."

His lips met hers in a deep, passionate kiss. Simone matched his intensity, thrilled to have him in her arms again.

"God, I've missed you!" he uttered before running his lips down her neck.

"I've missed you too. I still can't believe you're here."

They kissed again for what seemed like forever, taking their time to savor the moment. Simone marveled at the warm, sweet taste of his lips and the feel of his tongue. She let her hands explore the hard curves of his wide shoulders. When she ran her fingers over his chest and teased his flat nipples, Maxwell pulled his mouth away from hers and breathed in deep. Simone watched his jaw flex as his teeth clenched. Her eyes met his and she marveled at the fervor reflected in their inky depths. She held his hot gaze while her teasing touch took a slow, meandering path down his shirt.

"I guess you want that rain check now, huh?" she said.

Maxwell cracked a grin. "Yeah. Now would work."

Simone took his hand and led him into the apartment, stopping near the couch. She took his bag from his shoulder and dropped it on the up-holstered seat.

"Welcome to my apartment," she said, feeling almost shy to have him in her space.

Maxwell didn't even look around. His heated gaze was stuck on her face with an occasional glance down her body. "Show it to me later. Right now I want to do other things."

His voice was husky and deep. His implication left her breathless and tingly with anticipation. He pulled her into a kiss again, but now the chemistry between them was charged with electricity. Simone felt overwhelmed with need, and could not wait for romantic foreplay to take its course. She wanted Maxwell now.

Her hands went to his waistband and undid his belt with deft fingers. She could feel his heart pounding just as hard as hers. The sound of the harsh breathing filled the room. Then his zipper was down and her fingers stroked over his hard arousal as it strained against the cotton of his boxers.

Maxwell let out a harsh breath and kissed her again, sucking on her lips and tongue. Simone un-leashed his erection and wrapped her hand around its thickness. It felt hot and powerful against her palm. She ran her hand up and down its shaft. His lips trembled against hers while he whispered words of encouragement and adulation. She lengthened her strokes, giving special attention to the soft and sensitive tip.

He groaned deep in his throat, then covered her hand with his to stop her caresses. She felt him reach over the back of the couch, then riffle through his bag. When he pulled out a condom, Simone took it out of his hands and rolled on the thin sheath with gentle fingers.

With one swift movement, Maxwell took her waist in a solid grip and lifted her up to sit on the arm of the sofa. He stood between her parted legs and quickly undid the belt of her robe. The light, silky fabric fell open to reveal her full curves covered by delicate black underwear. Simone wrapped her legs around his hips, bringing their loins into contact.

"God, I want you so bad," he told her while brushing wet kisses along the upper swells of her breast. "I need you now, Simone!"

"Yes," she managed to utter breathlessly.

Maxwell brushed aside her panties and entered her body with one sure stroke. He withdrew, then plunged forward again, deeper. Simone moaned loudly as his rigid length filled her completely. It felt hot, intense, and overwhelming. Again and again, he thrust into her core with powerful strokes. She could only hold on to his shoulders and bite her lip to hold back her screams.

It was wild, unrestrained sex that had them sweating and panting. After weeks of missing him and wanting him, it was exactly what Simone needed.

"Maxwell!" she screamed when she couldn't hold back anymore. "God, Maxwell! Yes!"

"Come for me, Simone," he coached with a voice thick with arousal. "I want to watch you come."

Simone felt the familiar tingle start in her toes, creep up her legs, and explode between her thighs.

She fell apart, losing all awareness of her surroundings except the feel of Maxwell holding her close. Somewhere off in the distance, he joined her in climax, and their bodies remained deeply meshed. It was a beautiful completion.

"That wasn't exactly what I had planned," Maxwell stated with a cheeky grin.

He slid Simone off the sofa so she stood in front of him.

"Really? You didn't plan to ravage me without even removing your pants?" she shot back.

"What can I say? You seduced me with your hot body and sexy lingerie. I feel so used."

Simone slapped his shoulder lightly. They both laughed as they hugged.

"Come," she said when she took hold of his hand. "Let's go get cleaned up. I'll give you the real tour."

Maxwell picked up his bag and followed her through the living room and into the bedroom. Simone left him there to turn on the shower and grab two fresh bath towels. The two of them then spent long minutes under the water spray bathing and fooling around. When they finally returned to her bedroom, they slipped under the sheets, naked.

Simone cuddled up to Maxwell's side, and he wrapped an arm around her shoulder.

"We only have two full days together," she stated. "I don't want to waste them sleeping."

He pressed his lips on her forehead.

"I know," he agreed.

"So, what do you want to do? Now it's my turn to be the host."

"I'm pretty content right here. We might leave the bed to get some food, but that's about it."

"So you think you can live on sex and food, huh?"

"Yup. That's what heaven is all about," Maxwell replied.

"Well, I don't want you to overdose on the good stuff. So, how about we take a couple of breaks and get some fresh air?"

"If we have to."

Simone could hear the teasing smile in his voice. It was so hard to believe it was almost a month since they last saw each other. The way they spoke and interacted made it seem as though they had never been apart. Like the first time they had met, being with Maxwell felt comfortable and right. It wasn't anything she could explain, and Simone *had* tried to explain it over the last couple of months. It was just an intangible feeling.

"I didn't tell you, but when I couldn't reach you earlier, I ended up at Cedric's house," Maxwell stated.

"Cedric must have freaked out!" Simone said.

"Yeah, he was really surprised. Anyway, he and Amy invited us back over tomorrow for lunch. They're hoping my mom can make it as well."

"That's a great idea! Did you tell your mom you were in town?"

She felt him shake his head.

"No, not yet."

"Maxwell . . . !"

"I know, I know. It's just . . . It's a rough situation," he told her.

Simone's heart went out to him. Maxwell always seemed so strong and self-assured, but the circumstances with his mom and stepfather must still be hurtful.

"I know, Maxwell. But I'm sure she is going to be thrilled you're here. Don't you talk to her regularly?"

"She calls me every other week on Sunday. I don't call that house."

His words were so absolute that Simone was speechless for several seconds.

"Are you serious? Maxwell, that's horrible!"

"It is what it is, Simone."

"Well, it doesn't have to be that way," she insisted.

Maxwell took hold of her hand and brought it to his lips.

"Yes, it does," he replied softly. "I know I seem stubborn, Simone, but you don't know my stepfather."

She wanted to say something more, or ask him additional questions, but something in Maxwell's tone said he wasn't ready to delve into it further. So she let the matter drop and snuggled closer to his naked heat.

"So, what did you do tonight?" Maxwell asked a couple of minutes later.

"What?"

"Earlier, when I called from the airport," he clarified. "Where were you?"

Simone froze, trying to think of what to say and how she could avoid telling him the truth.

Chapter 23

Simone hadn't planned to see Kevin that evening. She was going to head home and start planning her next story with the online magazine. The last message from Kevin had been left earlier that week; she hadn't paid attention at the time since it was before she met Scott Claus, and there was no reason for her to call him back. All she remembered was him saying that he missed her and wanted to see her again, even as friends. Simone had finally gotten the nerve to return his call on Friday morning before her show. She left a message asking him to call her.

At around four o'clock that afternoon, Kevin did just that. Simone was driving up the interstate, a few minutes from home. The conversation was very brief. He asked her if she wanted to go to dinner later, and she immediately said yes. They agreed that Kevin would pick her up at seven o'clock, and that was it.

Simone could not believe it had been that easy. She didn't know what she expected, but in her mind, it would take a really cunning and calculated plan to get close to him again. For a moment, she felt a little deflated, but then panic quickly set in.

Instead of heading straight home, Simone stopped at a lingerie store in the mall. Feeling fortified in a new push-up bra and low-rise thong, she slipped into a slinky black dress with a low-cut neckline. When Kevin rang from downstairs, she stepped into sexy leather pumps, then sprayed perfume on her wrists and cleavage.

Her plan was simple. Simone was going to seduce Kevin into taking her back to his place. It couldn't be too hard, she told herself, since he had been trying to get into her pants for weeks. If he questioned her change of heart, she would just say she missed him, or realized that she made a mistake. But, knowing Kevin, he wouldn't think too deeply about it.

That was the whole scheme. She didn't have a clue what to do after they got to his apartment, so she just didn't think about it. Fortunately, Simone had been to Kevin's place twice before, so she knew the general layout, including the kitchen and his bathroom. If things worked out and they ended up there tonight, she would worry about the details then.

After the first brief greeting when Simone entered Kevin's car, there was little conversation until they were seated at their table. He had chosen a very swanky steak and sushi restaurant in Lennox Square.

"How have you been, Simone?" asked Kevin while they waited for their server to arrive.

"I'm all right," Simone replied.

"Good. I've been a little worried about you."

"Why?" she asked, genuinely surprised by his concern.

He shrugged nonchalantly. "You haven't returned any of my calls."

"That's because I told you I didn't want to go out anymore," she reminded him with a touch of sarcasm.

Kevin smirked, as though she had said something funny. "Yeah, but I knew you would get over whatever was bugging you."

"Are you saying that you didn't take me seriously?"

The smirk on his face grew to an arrogant grin. "You're here, aren't you?"

Simone looked down at the table, instantly remembering why she had no interest in a relationship with Kevin, despite his wealth and celebrity status. In that moment, she so wanted to tell him to go screw himself, but bit the side of her cheek instead.

When she looked back up, she tried to be charming.

"You're right. I'm here," she replied. "Congratulations, by the way. I heard you have a title match scheduled in the fall."

"Yeah," he said simply.

"I was really surprised. You never mentioned ending your retirement."

"It wasn't confirmed."

"So, how is it going now? When is the fight? It's in Vegas, right?" Simone questioned.

Kevin took the bait and starting talking about himself. She put on a fascinated expression and spent the next thirty minutes listening for any revealing information. He confirmed that the venue was in one of the large Las Vegas casinos, then talked about the media hype that surrounded his comeback. After this weekend, he would be on the road for a few weeks doing promotional events and interviews. Simone detected annoyance in his tone, and sensed he was a little frustrated with the whole thing.

"How is the training going?" she finally asked.

"Good," he said. "I'm a little heavier than I would like, but I'm working with it."

"How often do you have to train?"

"Every day. I'm in the gym for at least four hours a day."

"Wow," Simone gasped with wonder. "It must be hard to go back to that type of conditioning."

"Maybe at first, but I've always worked out, so it wasn't so bad."

Simone nodded. She couldn't think of anything else to say about the topic, so she let him go back to talking about the boxing industry. There was a small part of her that hoped he would say something revealing about using questionable supplements, or having trouble getting back in shape. Anything that would let her know this plan to find steroids in his possession was not a big waste of time.

The next time Simone checked her watch, it was almost nine o'clock. They had finished their meals a while ago and were just having another round of drinks. She had white wine and Kevin stuck to bottled water. Their table was approached several times by strangers, fans, or Kevin's acquaintances, all wanting to talk about the upcoming fight and wish him the best.

She smiled politely, but mostly remained quiet. In her mind, she was frantically trying to think of a way to get back to his apartment.

"Are you ready?" he finally asked.

Simone nodded, and followed him out of the restaurant. As they walked toward the underground parking, she stayed close to his side, smiling brightly and looking into his eyes whenever possible.

"So, where to now?" she asked once they were seated in the car and driving out of the building.

"I have to make an appearance at a club downtown soon," Kevin told her.

"Oh, that's too bad. I thought we could go back to your place for a little bit."

He turned his head to look at her hard, clearly surprised at the suggestion. Simone pursed her lips slightly, hoping she looked alluring.

"You can go to that club later, can't you?" she continued.

Kevin looked at the clock on the dashboard, then back at her. It was clear he was very interested and was considering the offer. "Why don't you come with me? Then, after I'm done, we'll have the whole night to ourselves."

Kevin put his hand on her thigh and squeezed her flesh. He looked hard at her lips, then down at her cleavage. She cringed inside, but kept the expression on her face seductive and beguiling.

There was no way she was going to go out clubbing with him. If Maxwell ever found out about it, Simone just knew he would never forgive her. It had been hard enough to explain that picture in the newspaper, never mind their argument last night about her seeing Kevin again to investigate the steroid use.

"I can't," she replied to his offer. "I have to be up really early tomorrow for an appointment."

"Come on. I'll make it worth your while."

His hand slid higher, going up her skirt. Simone covered it with hers, entwining their fingers to stop his movement.

"I'm sure you would, but maybe next time," she told him, trying hard to sound disappointed.

They were both silent while he made the short drive back to her building. Instead of stopping up in front of the lobby doors, Kevin drove around to the back and pulled into a visitor's parking spot. Simone's spine straightened with alarm.

He shut off the engine and reached across the car before she could stop him. His mouth pressed on hers, hard and invading, while both his hands dug at her inner thighs.

"There's no need to wait," he uttered between kisses. "We can go upstairs for a little bit."

His hands and mouth felt so foreign on her skin. Simone felt panic raise up in her throat, but tried to stay calm. What was she going to do? She had all but told him that this was what she wanted.

"We could, but wouldn't it be better to wait?" she whispered. "I don't like to rush."

Simone held her breath, hoping Kevin wouldn't notice that she was completely contradicting her earlier suggestion. Luckily, he was completely engrossed in biting at her neck and didn't appear to notice. His hands had moved up to her breasts, squeezing their full curves.

"I've waited long enough. Let's just go upstairs and do this," he mumbled. "Damn, your tits are nice!"

She squeezed her eyes tight and bit the side of her mouth. Finally, she couldn't take it anymore and pushed at his shoulders. It took a few seconds for him to get her message.

"What?" he demanded.

His eyes flashed with annoyance. Simone put a gentle hand on his shoulder, trying to placate him.

"We better stop. A car just pulled up next to us," she whispered.

There was no car, but Simone looked around as if trying to see where it went. Kevin let out a sharp breath.

"It's getting late, anyway," she continued. "I don't want you to be late for the club. Why don't you give me a call tomorrow?"

Before he could object, she opened the passenger door and stepped out of the vehicle. The look on Kevin's face revealed a mix of frustration and confusion. Simone smiled and waved before walking quickly to the building and entering through one of the back entrances.

Once inside, she stood in the hall with her breath coming in short pants as though she had been running. She waited a few minutes, then opened the door again to make sure Kevin hadn't come after her. Thankfully, his car was gone, so she made her way up to her apartment.

Maybe Maxwell was right and she should just walk away from this whole thing. Tonight had been a disaster and it was obvious that she had no clue how to go about this type of thing. In the end, she did not get any more information than she had before, and Kevin now thought she was a tease. She had managed to get away relatively unscathed, but what about next time? If she was successful and got into his apartment, how would she manage to avoid intimacy with him?

Simone was also disappointed with her emotional reaction. Kevin had not done anything more than he had while they were dating, so why did she feel so trashy? It felt horrible to know that she was using her body and the promise of sex to get what she wanted. It was a silly and childish sentiment for someone who wanted to be a journalist. She had better toughen up now or get out of the game.

After this weekend, Kevin was going to be out of town for a few weeks. What if he stopped taking the steroids by then? If she waited, she and Scott might never find out who Natasha's source had been, and who may have been responsible for her death.

There was no question that the plan had to go down this weekend.

Chapter 24

Now, a few hours later, Maxwell was naked with Simone in her bed. His eyes were closed as they lay wrapped in each other's arms with their fingers entwined. There were a few minutes of silence after they had discussed his mother. Maxwell didn't want the topic to come up again, so he deliberately changed the subject.

"Earlier, when I called from the airport, where were you?" he asked Simone.

"Oh. I had to meet a friend," she told him, but there had been a pause before the response.

Maxwell knew right away that something was wrong. He let go of her hand and rose onto his elbow to peer down at her face.

"Simone?"

She looked away, avoiding his gaze.

Immediately, he knew what she wasn't telling him.

"Damn it!" he exclaimed before rolling away from her and sitting up at the edge of the bed. "You went to see Kevin Johnson, didn't you?"

There was no need for her to confirm it. His back was to her, but Maxwell could feel her tension and hesitancy. When Simone finally responded, her voice was firm and unapologetic.

"Yes."

"God, Simone! I told you not to do it! It's too dangerous."

"And I told you that I had made a commitment and it was too late to back out. I'm the only one that can do this."

"So what? If Kevin wants to pop steroids and blow up like the Michelin Man, who cares?" Maxwell exclaimed.

"Doesn't it bother you he might be cheating? It's not right, Maxwell. Millions of people will be watching the fight, maybe even betting their money to see a fair competition. It's not right. If I turn a blind eye and do nothing, then I'm just as bad."

"That's a load of crap, Simone." His words sounded more harsh than he had intended. "Look, I get what you're trying to say. I respect your integrity. But you're not the police, Simone. You should not have to put yourself in danger to right someone else's wrong."

"Well, I'm sorry, but I don't see it that way."

Maxwell sat thinking for a long moment, trying to come up with the words that would penetrate her stubbornness. Something about this whole thing just did not make sense to him. Simone was not the type to seek out drama and confrontation just for the thrill of it, so what was her connection to this plan? He understood that her close friend died before she could confide in Simone. But he found it hard to believe all this was about fulfilling a project on Natasha's behalf. After all, Natasha was dating Kevin behind Simone's back. There had to be more to it.

"I don't get it, Simone. I don't think you're telling

me everything," he stated strongly. "What does any of this have to do with you? Why are you so hell-bent on getting involved in this? That reporter will get his big story. What do you get? Is this part of your effort to do more journalism work?"

Simone sighed loudly, and he heard her move off the bed. He watched as she walked across the room and pulled a white cotton baby doll out of the closet. She didn't respond to him until after she slipped it over her head.

"Maxwell, I think we're going to have to agree to disagree. I'm sorry you don't understand it," she replied softly. "Don't you want to know what happened tonight?"

It was his turn to sigh.

"I don't think I want to know," he told her.

"Nothing happened. I accepted his offer for dinner, we ate, and then he dropped me back home."

"That's it?"

"That's all," she confirmed.

"Good. So it's over, then."

Simone just gave him a blank stare, proving that his attempt at dry humor did not go over well. Maxwell stood up and walked over to her. They stood inches apart, both searching each other's eyes for some sign of capitulation.

"You're going to try again," Maxwell finally stated.

"Maxwell, I've already repeated to myself every objection that you have stated. I would love to walk away from this whole mess. And to be honest, I don't know how I'm going to pull it off. But I have to try," she explained passionately. "Part of me wants to prove that Kevin has nothing to do with those steroids, and that the truth about it died with Natasha."

Maxwell pulled her into his arms. He now saw that she was as fearful and hesitant about the investigation as he was. Yet she wasn't going to let that stop her. If he wasn't so frustrated by his inability to protect her, he would be proud of her tenacity and courage.

"Come, let's go back to bed," he urged.

Simone nodded and followed his lead.

"I'm so glad you're here," she told him once they were under the covers in the dark.

They fell asleep spooned tightly. Simone was already gone from the bed when he woke the next morning. He found her in the kitchen drinking a cup of coffee and watching the news.

"Good morning," he announced as he approached her.

She gave him a sweet smile and stepped into his arms.

"Did you sleep okay?" she asked.

"Better than I have since you left Toronto."

"Hmmm. I know how you feel."

"How long have you been up?" Malcolm wanted to know.

"Not long. Would you like some coffee?"

"Sure."

They broke apart. Simone went to prepare his cup, and Malcolm sat down at the breakfast bar.

"I just spoke with Amy," she stated while passing him a steaming hot mug. "She said we should come over any time after one o'clock this afternoon. Unfortunately, your mom can't make it."

Maxwell nodded. He immediately felt relieved and disappointed at the same time, but put it out of his mind. There was no way he was going to spend the day with Simone brooding about things he could not change.

"I have to do a couple errands downtown, so I was thinking we could head down there and get some breakfast," continued Simone.

"That sounds good," he told her.

"Is there anything you need to do? Do you want to go by College Park?"

"Nah, there's no one there that I need to see. Since I'm only here for the weekend, it doesn't make sense to tell anyone. I'll hook up with some friends next time."

Simone and Maxwell finished their coffee, then showered and dressed to head out. As she drove down the highway into the city's core, Maxwell marveled at all the changes to the landscape.

It was hard for him to believe that he had left the city over nine years ago. He had not gotten up to the north end of Atlanta often, but the large amount of development and new construction was still very dramatic. Maxwell thought back to Simone's offer to visit his old neighborhood. It would be interesting to see who was still around in College Park, and visit some of his old hangouts. He would do it on his next trip back.

He looked over at Simone, and marveled at her impact on his life. If there was any doubt about his feeling for her, this last-minute trip certainly clarified things. Maxwell was in love with her, thoroughly and completely, and would do anything to keep her safe. He also came to accept that it didn't matter where they lived as long as they were together. Toronto had become his new home, but a return to Atlanta now seemed like a reasonable option.

After breakfast, they spent a few hours in the city walking around and completing Simone's list of errands. It was almost three o'clock in the afternoon when they reached Amy and Cedric's house.

"So, everything's cool with you and Simone?" Cedric asked him sometime later. "You guys seem pretty tight."

The girls were in the kitchen while the brothers were watching a baseball game in the den. They were drinking from bottles of cold beer and snacking on potato chips.

"It's good," Maxwell replied. "I'm not enjoying the long-distance thing, but other than that, it's really good."

Cedric chuckled for a second. "Amy is convinced that she and Simone are going to be sisters-in-law. She's even started flipping through her bridal magazines again. I told her not to get her hopes up. It's only been a few months."

Maxwell smiled a bit and took a sip from his drink.

"Amy could be right," he replied softly.

His baby brother looked shocked for a moment, his mouth hanging open as he stared at Maxwell. "You're serious!"

"Maybe not right away," Maxwell told him. "But I would like to see that happen sometime in the future."

"So she's the one, huh?"

Maxwell nodded slowly and with certainty.

"Yup, she's the one, Cedric."

"What will you do? Move back to Atlanta?" he asked, echoing the thoughts that had run through Maxwell's mind all day.

"I don't know. It's possible."

Cedric looked at him hard and assessing for a long moment.

"When Mom told me she couldn't come by today, I told her you were here. She started crying, Maxwell."

"Ahhh, Cedric. Why did you have to do that?"

"Listen, just listen. I spoke to Dad too. They want to know if you can come by the house tomorrow. Maxwell, he wants to talk to you and sort this stuff out."

"No."

The answer was hard and absolute.

"Maxwell, it's time, man. I'm not saying Dad has changed or mellowed with age or something. He's the same hard-ass he always was, and I doubt he will change. But that doesn't mean he's not ready to fix things between the two of you. The least you can do is meet him halfway."

"I don't have to do anything, Cedric. There is nothing to fix."

"Damn it! Why do you have to be so stubborn, Max? Why does it have to be all or nothing? Can't you at least do it for Mom? She's the one that's really hurting."

Maxwell drank his beer without responding. Cedric sighed with frustration, but let the matter drop.

The men went back to watching the game in silence. Amy and Simone joined them later and they hung out as a group for another hour. Though they were invited to stay for dinner, Maxwell and Simone decided to see a movie and grab a quick meal near the theater.

They were waiting in line to purchase their tickets when Maxwell's cell phone rang. He recognized his mom's home number right away, so he moved a few steps away to answer it in private, leaving Simone to hold their spot.

"Hello, Maxwell. It's your father."

Chapter 25

Maxwell was caught completely off guard. It took him a few long seconds before he could decide how to respond.

"Maxwell?" repeated Thomas Smith.

"Yes, I'm here."

"I'll get right to the point. Cedric let us know you are in town. Your mother and I would like you to come by the house tomorrow. To talk."

The last two words were added after a slight hesitation.

Maxwell looked over to Simone waiting for him, clearly interested about his need to take the call in private.

"That's not possible. I'm busy tomorrow," he finally replied.

"I'm sure you can spare a few minutes. Cedric can drive you over."

It was clear that he wasn't asking, and his arrogance made Maxwell want to give him a few choice words and hang up the phone. But this situation was much bigger than his stepfather. It always had been, but Maxwell had been too pigheaded and selfish to really see it before. Cedric and his mom did not deserve to be in the middle of this situation.

"What time?" he finally asked.

"Your mother has a church meeting in the afternoon, so we won't be home until around four thirty. Let's say five o'clock."

"All right. I'll let Cedric know."

"Good," his stepfather said.

The call ended shortly after. Maxwell immediately called his brother and relayed the information. Cedric quickly agreed to pick him up at Simone's apartment.

"Is everything okay?" inquired Simone when he returned to her.

Maxwell had already decided to wait until after the movie to tell her the details. She had just finished purchasing their movie tickets. He nodded in response to her question, but changed the subject.

"What theater are we in?" he asked instead.

She checked the ticket and they made their way to the correct screening.

The film was a new comedy, and judging from the waves of laughter in the audience, it was pretty good. Unfortunately, Maxwell's mind was on other things and he could barely follow the plot. He thought he was doing a pretty good job of appearing unruffled, but Simone set him straight on the way back to her place.

"What's the matter, Maxwell? You've been a little quiet since we left Amy and Cedric's place."

"It's nothing, really."

"Is everything okay?" she persisted.

"Yeah," Maxwell replied while letting out a long sigh. "Did you have anything planned for tomorrow?"

"No. Why?"

"My stepfather called earlier. Cedric told them

I was in town and they want both of us to come by the house tomorrow."

"That's great, Maxwell. You *are* going, right?"

"I told him I would," he confirmed.

Even though he tried to squash the resentment he felt, Maxwell knew it was obvious in his tone. Simone glanced at him and her concern was evident.

"It's not a big deal," he added. "The whole thing has gone on too long. I'm here, so I might as well see if the situation can be improved. It can't get much worse."

"True," she said.

"I'm just sorry it will take away from our time together. That's not what I intended."

"Maxwell, don't worry about it. What time are you guys going?"

"Cedric's going to pick me up after four o'clock. I'll only be gone a couple of hours," he predicted earnestly.

"That's fine. You have to stay for as long as it takes. It's important."

Simone had just parked her car in the underground lot. She turned to face him and put a reassuring hand on his thigh.

"Think of it this way," she added with a teasing smile. "If things go well, you'll have to come to Atlanta more often."

Maxwell put his hand over hers and entwined their fingers.

"I plan to do that anyway," he told her.

"Really?"

"Really."

He leaned forward and ran his lips over hers, stoking the fire that was always smoldering between them.

"Simone, I'm in love with you."

His forehead was pressed against hers, and the words tumbled out before he could hold them back.

"It feels like I have loved you since the minute I pulled you out of that pool. I know it's crazy, but—"

"Maxwell," she interrupted, pulling back to meet his eyes. "I feel the same way. I love you too."

He kissed her again, his eyes closed tight with relief.

"God, I can't even remember my life before I met you, Simone. I know the situation is complicated. You here, me in Toronto. But it will work out, I promise."

"I know, Maxwell."

They sat in the car kissing and hugging until he suggested they head upstairs and finish what had been started.

As always, their lovemaking was intense and overwhelming. Once inside the apartment, Maxwell guided her to the bedroom, leaving a trail of discarded clothing behind. When he gently laid her back on the bed, they were both naked and panting hard. Kneeling on the floor, he ran his hands up and down her legs with light, massaging strokes. Maxwell then picked up one of her feet, and using his lips and tongue, he traveled a path over her toes and ankles, up the calves and thighs. The journey ended with his lips tracing the tender spot at the apex of her thighs.

Maxwell dipped a little lower, using his tongue to tease the edges of her feminine folds.

"Maxwell," she murmured huskily.

He pushed her legs apart slightly and delved deeper to taste her sweet nectar. Simone moaned softly, quivering every time he probed her tight cleft. Maxwell widened her thighs farther and buried his mouth between them, devouring the inner contours of her mound. Her body arched from the intensity of the assault while she panted his name over and over again until she climaxed dramatically.

Maxwell joined her on the bed, and paused for a moment to look down at her beautiful eyes, dark with spent passion. Her full lips trembled with every breath. He ran his fingers over the swells of her breasts, and the chestnut-colored skin felt like silk under his fingers.

"What?" she asked, still drowsy from her pleasure.

"I could look at you forever, Simone."

She lifted herself up onto one elbow, holding his gaze.

"I hope you plan to do more than look," she quipped.

Maxwell pulled her close and positioned himself between her legs before replying to her banter. "It's a good thing I can multitask."

Their teasing smiles faded as he slowly, steadily filled her with his arousal. With a firm hold on her bottom with one hand, Maxwell took them on a long, vigorous ride. He felt so good encased in her tight sheath. It took every ounce of his strength to prolong their time together, allowing their arousal to build to a breathtaking peak. Finally, when Simone's body tightened over his with the soft waves of completion, he let himself go. As always with her, the orgasm was overwhelming, leaving him breathless and completely spent.

"I love you," he whispered, holding her tight with his face pressed into the curve of her shoulder.

"I love you too."

Simone and Maxwell slept in the next morning, but managed to get out of the apartment before eleven o'clock. They had Sunday brunch at the Ritz Carlton in Midtown, then walked over to Sweet

Auburn to browse around like tourists. It was an idyllic afternoon spent holding hands and strolling aimlessly. Simone found herself constantly glancing over at Maxwell to admire his handsome profile, his solid broad shoulders, or the way he filled out his jeans. She felt as though she were walking on clouds, particularly after what they had shared the night before.

It certainly made her plans for the evening even harder to stomach.

Later that afternoon, Maxwell and Cedric left to go to their parents' house as planned. Simone told them to take their time and gave Maxwell a spare key in case she was out when they returned. The minute the door closed behind them, she dashed into the bathroom to take a quick shower. Just to be cautious, she waited another fifteen minutes before getting dressed again. The last thing Simone wanted was for Maxwell to return unexpectedly and find her getting dolled up for another date with Kevin Johnson.

After she had rushed out of Kevin's car on Friday evening, he had called her four times, but only left two messages on Saturday. He wanted to see her again that weekend. Now that she had successfully reconnected with Kevin, Simone really wanted the whole thing over and done with as quickly as possible. But since Maxwell arrived, it did not seem possible for her to get away, and she was afraid that she would miss the opportunity to see Kevin again before he left town.

That phone call from Maxwell's stepfather was a stroke of luck. It gave Simone a window of opportunity that she could not pass up. She called Kevin back late Saturday night, while Maxwell slept soundlessly after their lovemaking.

Kevin had suggested coming by her place, but

Simone claimed she would be downtown all day
and it would be easier for her to stop by his condo.
He agreed in the end.

If everything worked out well, she would be back
home before Maxwell even knew she went out.
Simone knew she would eventually tell him what
she had done, but only after they had spent the rest
of their time together. Then the thing with Kevin
would be over one way or the other, and no longer
a factor in their life.

By the time she arrived at Kevin's building,
Simone was not as nervous and panicked as on
Friday. Knowing that Maxwell was there in the city,
and would be with her later, made the whole thing
much easier to bear.

Kevin opened the door to his penthouse condo
wearing long, loose gym shorts that rode low on
his hips. He was on the phone, so just nodded to
her silently and motioned for her to enter. Simone
gave him a pleasant smile before trailing in behind
him. The apartment looked the same as she remembered: a man's pad with lots of electronics
and black leather chairs.

"Sorry about that," Kevin said after hanging up
the phone.

He hugged her loosely and pressed a quick kiss
on her lips.

"That's okay," she assured him.

"Do you want something to drink?"

"Sure. Wine would be nice."

Kevin disappeared into the kitchen. She could
hear him rumbling around in the cupboards.

"I've found some red wine. Is that okay? I think
it was a gift, or something," he shouted.

Simone joined him in the kitchen and put her
purse down on the counter.

"Anything is fine," she told him.

He went to work uncorking the bottle, and she slipped onto one of the stools in front of his breakfast bar. He handed her a glass a moment later.

"Are you hungry?" he asked. "I ordered some food earlier."

She shook her head. "No, I'm okay. I had a big lunch."

Simone sipped her drink while watching him dig into take-out containers from a local restaurant. Once his plate was full of fried chicken and rice, he went into the living room and sat down on the couch. Simone followed him silently and sat beside him. The large flat-screen television was already on, tuned into a sports channel. Kevin became immediately engrossed in the broadcast, eating without looking at the plate.

As the minutes ticked by in silence, it became harder for Simone to sit still. She drank her wine more quickly than usual, trying hard not to appear anxious. Her mind worked hard to figure out how she could look around the apartment without getting caught.

I should start in the kitchen cupboards, she thought, then drained the rest of her drink.

Unfortunately, Kevin had just finished his dinner and stood up suddenly, his empty plate in hand.

"I'll take that," he said, plucking the cup out of her hand and taking it into the kitchen for her.

Simone closed her eyes shut and hung her head with momentary defeat.

He was back a moment later with a bottle of water in his hand. "Let's go into the bedroom."

Chapter 26

She stood up and went with him.

Kevin shared the spacious two-bedroom condo with his brother, Donald. He led Simone to the only room at the end of a short hallway. She had a moment to look around the master suite with a full bathroom near the entrance. Donald's bedroom must be at the other end of the apartment, she thought.

"Come here," Kevin commanded.

He had stopped near the head of the king-sized bed, and put his water down on the side table. Simone did as he asked and allowed him to pull her into a deep kiss.

"Hmmm," she sighed, pulling away the second it felt appropriate, and giving him a teasing glance through her lashes. "Do you mind if I use your bathroom?"

Kevin kissed her again and rubbed his pelvis against her lower stomach. His erection was hard and very evident.

"I'll just be a second," Simone added.

Reluctantly, he released her. By the time she

closed the bathroom door, he was stepping out of
his shorts and ready to climb onto the bed.

"Okay, okay, okay," she panted in a whisper.
"Okay. You can do this."

After a few seconds of rapid breathing, Simone
got to work searching the bathroom. The medicine cabinet had a variety of painkillers, creams,
and toiletries, but nothing that looked like diet
supplements or performance enhancers.

A quiet riffle through the drawers and lower cab-
inets also did not produce anything.

Simone leaned against the counter and took a
deep breath.

"Hey, are you okay?" Kevin yelled though the door.

"I'll be out in a sec," she replied.

Desperately, Simone reopened the cabinet and went
through the medicine bottles again. She checked
every container by pouring the contents into her hand
to make sure the pills she sought weren't stashed in
them. Everything looked legit, so she carefully put
things back the way she found them.

After one last look around, Simone reentered the
bedroom. Kevin lay naked on top of his bed,
propped up on a pillow and watching a small
plasma screen mounted on the opposite wall. "What
took you so long? I was starting to get worried
about you."

"Sorry," she told him sweetly. "My stomach started
hurting. I don't know what it is."

He looked away from the television and his face
showed concern. "Are you okay?"

"I'm not sure."

"Come," Kevin urged, patting the spot on the bed
next top him. "I have a way to make you feel better."

Simone walked to him, pretending to be interested in what he was offering. His unclothed body

was pretty impressive, completely conditioned with thick, lean muscles. He was in excellent physical condition, but the sight of his naked body did nothing for her.

She sat beside him and ran a hand over her lower belly.

"Oh," she moaned.

"Have some of my water," Kevin offered.

"Do you have antacids or something? I think the wine gave me heartburn."

"I don't know. There might be some in the kitchen," he suggested. "I'll go check for you."

"No!" shouted Simone. "No, that's okay. I'll go. I think walking will help."

"Are you sure?"

"Yup."

He shrugged and went back to watching the television.

Simone walked out of the room, rubbing her stomach at the spot just below the rib cage. When she got to the kitchen, it took a little searching before she found the right shelf. It was beside the fridge, above the mishmash of juice glasses, and had a few typical household medicines. She shoved aside cold syrup, seasonal allergy pills, peroxide, and a box of Band-Aids. There was a bottle of chewable antacid tablets at the very back. Simone took it out just in case.

She closed the cupboard.

That's it, she thought. *There's nothing here.* Unless Kevin had those pills hidden in his bedroom, or somewhere else, there was a good chance Natasha had not gotten them from him.

Feeling relieved and better than she had in days, Simone turned around to head back to the room. That's when she saw the bottle beside the sink.

The name TRIAFUEL was spelled out in large letters across the front. It was the same name that was printed on the capsule in the picture that Scott Claus had shown her.

Simone froze for a second, then put down the antacids. She took a deep breath and looked around the apartment nervously. When she finally picked up the Triafuel, the label described it as an all-natural vitamin supplement and recommended a dose of one pill three times a day with meals. She removed the lid and poured some of the contents into her palm. They were definitely the steroids, and the bottle was about half-empty.

Without stopping to think, Simone pushed two of the capsules into the underside of her bra. She replaced the cap to the container and was about to put it back on the counter.

"Hey."

Simone whipped around toward the voice, the bottle still in her hand but slightly behind her, hidden from view.

"Donald! You scared me," she gasped, placing her empty hand on her chest to emphasize fright.

"Sorry," he replied as he walked farther into the kitchen and opened the refrigerator. "I'm surprised to see you here. I thought you and Kevin broke up."

He didn't sound like he expected a response, and she was too preoccupied to reply, trying to figure out how to replace the bottle of steroids. Facing the sink again, Simone inched her hand up slowly and slipped the bottle onto the counter. She tried to push it back to the spot where she had found it without making a sound.

"What are you doing?" Donald demanded.

She jumped and whipped around. "What?"

Donald grabbed her arm with a tight grip.

"What are you doing?" he asked again with his face just a couple of inches from hers.

"Nothing! Let go of me!"

"What are you doing here? Where's Kevin?"

"I said let go of me!" Simone stated again, tugging at her arm to loosen his hold.

"Hey! What's going on?" Kevin asked as he entered the room dressed again in his shorts.

"Kevin, I told you this bitch was trouble!" replied Donald, still holding on to Simone.

He pulled her out of the kitchen with him to approach his brother.

"Donald—"

Simone interrupted them with outrage. "What the hell is your problem, Donald? Let go of me, now!"

He finally released her, and she quickly went to stand behind Kevin.

"She had those damn supplements, Kevin," Donald stated.

"I don't know what he's talking about, Kevin," she insisted. "I was just about to take the antacids, and he flipped out."

"The bitch is lying," accused Donald, and he lunged at her. "She was trying to steal the pills and I caught her."

Simone flinched and took a step back, but Kevin stepped between them.

"Donald, chill out!" he commanded. "She has an upset stomach, that's it."

Donald snickered and looked at Kevin with disgust.

"Damn it, Kevin! Don't you see what's going on?" Donald yelled.

"Look," intervened Simone. "I don't know what's going on here, but it's time for me to go."

Holding her breath, she quickly walked past the two men, grabbing her purse while heading for the door.

"I don't think so."

Donald snatched her purse out of her hand, dragging her backward in the process. Simone stumbled and almost fell, but used one of the stools to steady herself. She watched in horror as Donald opened her purse and emptied the contents on the breakfast bar. Kevin looked back and forth between them, clearly uncertain of what to do.

"Stop that!" she yelled. "Give me back my things!"

"Shut up, bitch!"

"Donald, man, this is crazy. What are you looking for?" Kevin asked.

"I told you she was trouble, just like her skanky friend. But you just don't listen, Kevin. You just don't get it."

"Donald! You're acting crazy, man."

Donald threw the empty bag on the floor and looked at his brother with disgust.

"You just don't get it, do you?" he spat at Kevin before he stormed away.

Simone and Kevin looked at each other as a door slammed nearby. She took a deep breath, then started to pick up her stuff.

"Are you okay?" Kevin finally asked her. "Did he hurt you?"

"No."

"Look, I'm really sorry. Donald's been a little stressed out lately. This whole comeback fight has been more complicated than we planned."

Simone finally had her stuff together and put

her purse over her shoulder. The two pills she took were digging into the underside of her breast.

"What supplements is he talking about, Kevin? Why would he think I would take them?"

"I don't know. Just forget it."

She looked into his eyes and saw only confusion mixed with frustration. "I better go."

He didn't object and walked her to the door.

"I'm leaving in the morning. I'll call you," he promised.

She nodded and whispered good-bye.

The walk out of his building seemed to take forever. Simone didn't breathe until she was outside the front door of the lobby, continuously checking over her shoulder. She pulled her cell phone out of her purse and called Maxwell. The digital clock indicated it was six thirty, only two hours since Maxwell had left her house with Cedric.

He didn't answer, so she left a message.

"Maxwell, it's me. Give me a call when you get this. I'll be home in about fifteen minutes."

Simone paused, then plunged forward before she could change her mind.

"Please don't be mad, but I went to Kevin's place. The steroids are his, Maxwell, and I was able to get proof. Anyway, it's over now. Call me when you get this message."

Just saying the words made her feel so much better. Things had not gone exactly as planned, but in the end, it was successful. Simone had gotten the evidence she sought, and learned a lot about the relationship between Kevin and his brother.

The worst part of the whole fiasco was lying to Maxwell and sneaking around behind his back. No matter how much she wished she never had to tell

Maxwell what she did, she hated the thought of lying to him.

It *was* over. Tomorrow, she would call Scott and give him what she found. The rest was out of her hands. Clearly, Kevin was in a bad situation, and Simone wondered if he was completely aware of everything going on around him. He trusted Donald as his manager and brother, and his trust appeared to be a mistake.

Simone took a deep breath of warm night air before continuing the walk to her car. She started thinking about how she and Maxwell could spend their last evening together. After another shower, she planned to put on something really sexy, light some candles, and wait for his return. She unlocked her car door, already smiling with anticipation.

The arm that wrapped around her midsection caught her completely by surprise. A large, rough hand covered her mouth before she could scream.

Simone struggled wildly, trying to break free, but it was no use. The man who held her was too big and too strong.

"Stop struggling or I will snap your neck. Do you understand?" he stated in a harsh voice.

She nodded, holding her breath.

"Good. Now, be a good girl and give me the keys."

Chapter 27

Maxwell and Cedric didn't say much on the drive to their parents' home. Thomas and Dolores Smith had moved out of College Park about seven years ago, and now lived north of Atlanta in Marietta. Dolores had told Maxwell all about the new house, but this was his first time there. It was about twenty miles away from Simone's apartment, and the brothers arrived a few minutes before five o'clock.

"They're home," Cedric stated as they turned into the driveway and parked next to their father's late-model Cadillac. "Are you ready?"

"As ready as I'll ever be," Maxwell replied flippantly.

Their mom answered the door still wearing her pretty yellow church dress, and immediately pulled Maxwell into a deep hug. He felt her slender frame tremble with emotion, and his throat tightened with the threat of tears in his eyes.

"Hey, hey. Don't I get some sugar too, Mama?" Cedric finally asked

Dolores finally pulled away from her firstborn son with a smile of pure joy on her face. She hugged Cedric also.

"It's so good to see you boys together," she told

them. "Come inside. Are you hungry? There's a pot of oxtail on the stove."

"No," replied Maxwell.

"I'll have a little taste," Cedric said.

They followed her through the house passing a formal sitting area and a dining room. She led them into the kitchen, and the boys took seats at the small round table in front of a pretty bay window. Maxwell recognized the wooden table right away, and ran his hand over the worn and scuffed surface. It had been the center of all the activity at their old house in College Park.

Maxwell watched as his mom served Cedric a generous plate of tender oxtail on a bed of rice and peas. It was like hundreds of past meals from his youth.

"How long are you going to be in Atlanta, son?" Dolores asked as she put a tall glass of lemonade in front of Maxwell.

"I'm leaving tomorrow, Mom." Her disappointment was very evident on her face. "But I'll be back soon."

She smiled, nodding as she gently placed her hand over his. "Your father will be down in a minute."

"Mom, what's this about? What's going on?" Maxwell finally asked.

"It's time to end this foolishness."

The austere statement came from the entrance of the kitchen. Dolores's hand tapped Maxwell's, but she looked to her husband as he entered the room. His expression was hard and unreadable.

Maxwell tried to remain relaxed and unaffected, but his spine immediately straightened. His teeth clenched hard, causing his jaw to protrude aggressively.

"Cedric," Thomas said, laying a hand on his son's head.

"Hey, Pop," replied Cedric while chewing on his food.

He looked back and forth between his father and his brother, then back down to his plate.

Dolores stood up just as her husband sat in the last chair available around the table, beside Cedric and across from Maxwell. "Are you ready for dinner, Thomas?"

He nodded, but his eyes remained fixed on his stepson. The two men remained in a stare-down for several seconds. The only sound in the room came from pot lids clattering as Dolores fixed Thomas's plate.

"Do you want a beer?" Thomas finally asked.

The question was aimed at Maxwell with a gesture at the lemonade still untouched in front of him. Maxwell's brows lowered with momentary confusion. He looked closer at Thomas again, taking in the very gray hair and the web of lines under his eyes. Further signs of age were visible around his mouth and under his loose chin. He suddenly seemed more tired than harsh.

He shook his head and lowered his eyes.

"No, I'm good," he finally replied.

"So, you've come home, finally," stated Thomas.

His tone implied that this visit to Atlanta was somehow about Thomas and their altercation all those years ago. It made Maxwell bristle with resentment.

"I'm only here until tomorrow," he said, keeping his tone neutral.

Thomas nodded.

"Well, it was long overdue," his mom interjected as she put her husband's dinner in front of him. "Right, Thomas?"

He looked at Maxwell, but began eating his food instead of responding.

"Are your sure you're not hungry, baby?" Dolores asked Maxwell again.

She sat beside him with her own dinner.

"I'm all right, Mom. I had brunch not long ago."

The family sat quietly for several minutes. Cedric stared hard at his brother over their parents' heads, his eyes urging him to say something. Maxwell looked back with a blank stare.

"All right, Pop," Cedric finally said with frustration. "Maxwell is here. Why don't you say what you want to say?"

"Can I finish my dinner?" Thomas snapped back.

Cedric shrugged, clearly unfazed by his father's bluster. "Sure, go ahead. Why don't we wait another nine years for you to apologize?" he added.

Maxwell raised a brow, surprised at Cedric's sarcastic and disrespectful tone. But their father just snickered and went back to eating, while Cedric shared an amused smile with their mother.

This was not the family that Maxwell remembered. He looked around the table feeling like a complete stranger in a foreign environment. Cedric never talked back to Pops, and Mom would not laugh at her husband's expense. In the many times that he imagined being back at home, Maxwell had never envisioned that things would be different than they were when he was younger.

Finally, Thomas scraped up the last of his rice and put his fork down on the empty plate. He took a long drink of lemonade, then leaned back in his chair and looked back and forth between his sons.

"You two were so different as boys, it was like night and day," he finally stated. "Cedric, you were always so happy and eager to please. Your Mom and I never had to ask you to do anything twice. But, Maxwell, you rebelled constantly, questioning everything and everyone. You were so stubborn. Once you had made up your mind, that was it. Nothing or no one was going to change it."

Maxwell had heard enough. He pushed back his chair, ready to walk out of the room.

"Baby, wait," his mom said in a quiet voice.

The pleading in her eyes made him stay seated, though his fists remained clenched tight.

"It took me a long time to acknowledge that you were right. I did treat you boys different," Thomas stated softly.

He looked straight at Maxwell. His face was serious, but there was no hint of criticism or condemnation. "I did what I thought was best to raise you right, and that meant that I had to be hard on you, Max. It may have seemed unfair, but it was necessary. It was because I loved you."

The words hung in the air like a fog. Maxwell felt them all looking at him, judging his reaction to his father's words. He was so surprised, he didn't know how to respond.

"Do you remember that time you decided to make a fort in the backyard?" his father continued. "I woke up one morning and found you building this huge thing, and I couldn't believe it. I think you were nine years old, and you had half of it built before ten o'clock."

"You were pretty pissed that I had taken your tools," Maxwell finally said.

"Nah, it wasn't tools," Thomas replied. "I tried to explain that to you at the time, but you weren't hearing me. You had found the plans in a library book, and had somehow managed to get everything you needed. I just couldn't understand why you didn't come to me about it. We could have done it together. The minute I questioned you,

you threw down the hammer and stomped away.
Then I saw everything in the garbage by the curb
the next morning."

Thomas shook his head, still clearly affected by
the memory. Maxwell also remembered that day
clearly, but his version was very different. It was in
the last week before school started, and Maxwell had
spent most of the summer in Jamaica with his grandparents. While there, he had helped one of the
neighbors build a small shed. That's where he had
gotten the idea of building a fort in the backyard.

Maxwell had spent several days walking around
the neighborhood collecting scrap wood and other
materials to build his fort, and had stashed it all in
the far corner of the yard. Everything was ready on
Saturday morning, and he was up at dawn, convinced he could have it done before Pops woke up.

He had felt certain that his father would never
help him build the fort and would probably say no
to the idea altogether. So Maxwell decided to do it
on his own, reasoning that once it was up and Pops
saw how cool it was, he would let him keep it.

The project had been much harder than he had
anticipated, and by the time Pops found out about
it, Maxwell was frustrated and close to tears. Pops
immediately started yelling, and in his eyes, Maxwell
thought it was about using the tools without permission and the mess he had created. He had run away
before Pops could see him cry with bitter disappointment.

They never spoke about it again. The next summer,
Pops built a fort for Cedric. Maxwell refused to step
foot in it, no matter how much his younger bother
begged him.

"I thought that you would be excited when I
finally built one for you guys," Thomas continued

as though reading Maxwell's mind. "But you had no interest."

"I remember that," Cedric threw in, looking at his brother. "You kept saying you were too old to play with me in it."

"It was your fort, not mine," replied Maxwell.

"It was for both of you, Max," their father stated. "I was trying to make up for not helping you with yours."

Maxwell realized now that he might have interpreted the situation wrong. The whole thing seemed so childish now, but at the time, it had hurt so much. And there were so many other instances when he judged his father's actions as evidence of favoritism toward his real son. Was he wrong?

"Son, you're a grown man now," Thomas continued. "You understand that men sometimes say things out of jealousy and anger. Things they don't mean, and don't know how to take back. I know I have let this thing go on for too long. We both have because we are both very stubborn. But it's time to end it."

Maxwell looked into the eyes of the man that he had tried to please for most of his life. To a young man, those eyes and his words always seemed to be filled with criticism, condemnation, and disappointment. None of those things were there now. There was only earnest appeal and honesty.

"Pop," Maxwell said, then paused with surprise. "I knew you weren't my father, but for a long time I wanted to feel like your son. I never did. You looked at Cedric like he was your whole world, and you looked at me as a nuisance and troublemaker."

"That wasn't my intention," Thomas insisted.

"Maybe not, but it doesn't change the way things were."

"Maxwell, you have to understand that you and Cedric were different people. At seven years old, you were so mature it was like living with another man in the house. I didn't know how to deal with that."

"It's true, baby," his mom added with laughter in her eyes. "You were always such a serious and willful boy. I don't even remember you crying past the age of three years old."

Maxwell knew their words were true. Friends and family were always telling him to lighten up and smile a little. He saw now that he spent so much time being resentful and sullen that he must have been a hard child to get close to.

"You are both my sons," his father said softly.

"That day I left—"

"Your mother and I had been arguing," Thomas interrupted. "She wanted to send April back to Detroit and I refused. The things I said to you were really directed at her. I'm not proud of it, son, and I've paid for my callousness a hundred times over. I never meant a word of it, but these things happen in relationships."

As though sensing the turmoil in Maxwell's heart, his mother put a gentle hand on his arm.

"Baby, it's time for us to move on. I don't want us to live like this anymore," she pleaded.

Maxwell looked around at his family, letting go of the image he had carried inside for so long, and seeing them as the people they were today. He was suddenly filled with the need to know more about them than his mother could provide in their brief Sunday afternoon conversations.

"Hey, Pops," Cedric chimed in. "Do you remember the time that Max snuck out that night with your brand-new Chrysler LeBaron?"

Thomas's brows lowered, and his eyes blazed

with anger. It was the same expression he had when he caught Maxwell trying to put the keys to the car back in Pops's pocket before they were missed.

Cedric snorted before he burst out laughing. Dolores started to chuckle and it became impossible for Maxwell to hold back his own amusement.

For the next hour or so, Cedric delighted in taunting his dad with every one of Maxwell's escapades that he could think of, and there were many. They were all laughing so loud that Maxwell didn't hear his phone ring. He finally listened to Simone's message while he and Cedric were on their way back to her apartment.

Chapter 28

"Please," begged Simone. "You don't want to do this."

"Shut up!"

She suddenly felt the unmistakable coldness of a gun pressed hard against her rib cage.

"Give me the keys. We're going for a ride."

Helpless with fear and disbelief, she did as he demanded. Kevin then opened the door and shoved her into the front seat of the car. The barrel of the gun was aimed right at her head.

"Move over," he commanded.

Simone scrambled over the center console until she was in the passenger seat. Her hand immediately went to the lever, ready to open the door and jump out.

"Don't be stupid!" he snapped as he sat in her seat. "You'd be dead before your foot touched the ground."

She held her breath and closed her eyes tight.

"Please, Kevin. You don't know what you're doing."

"No! *You* don't know who you're messing with, Simone. Now, shut the hell up!"

Biting her lip, she looked around wildly as he

turned on the car and started to drive away. The evening sun still shone bright, but there was no one around. Once they were on the street, she looked at every car they passed, hoping that someone would see the fear in her eyes and do something to save her. Kevin still had the gun in his hand, though it was concealed under the loose jersey he wore. But it was enough to keep her sitting as still and as silent as possible.

He didn't say a word to her until he stopped the car behind an abandoned commercial building several miles away.

"Natasha told you about the pills, didn't she?"

Simone's eyes widened. She shook her head feverishly in denial. "I don't know what you're talking about!"

"Yes, you do. You know exactly what I'm talking about."

"No, you're wrong."

"Damn it, Simone! You couldn't leave it alone, could you? Now I have to take care of you too! Damn it!"

"No, Kevin. You're wrong. Natasha didn't tell me anything. I never spoke to her," she stated again, pleading for him to believe her. "She died by accident. God, please tell me that it was an accident, Kevin!"

Her voice broke into a sob.

"Donald was right. You were nothing but trouble from the beginning. I should have kicked you to the curb a long time ago. Then that bitch, Natasha, offered herself to me like a gift. She wasn't even my type, but I recognized her right away from that picture in your living room. I should have known she was up to no good, but I thought it would be funny to screw your friend while you acted like your ass

was gold. I didn't even know she was a reporter until
I saw it in the news."

He looked at Simone with disgust and pure fury.

"You played me, Simone. You sent her to de-
stroy me."

Simone couldn't believe what he was saying.

"No, Kevin, it's not like that. I swear I didn't even
know you had met Natasha."

"Stop lying!" he shouted, slamming his fist on
the dashboard.

She jumped, biting her lip to hold back the
scream that bubbled up in her throat.

"Do you know what's riding on this fight? Millions
of dollars, Simone. This fight is going to set me and
Donald up for the rest of our lives. Once I win the
belt again, it won't matter that the dealership is
going under. Nothing will matter. I just needed a
little boost, that's all. Just something to help me
train faster. It didn't hurt nobody."

Simone listened to his ranting, her eyes growing
wider with every word.

"Kevin, listen to me. We can fix this."

"It's too late, Simone. There's too much at stake.
I tried to tell Donald I wasn't ready. But he just
kept telling me to train harder. It's not that easy! I
just needed a little help."

He took a deep breath, then lifted the gun again,
pointing it at her head. "Get out of the car."

His tone made it clear that the conversation was
over. Simone saw the resolve in his eyes, and knew
that if she didn't get away now, he was going to
kill her.

She had spent the last few seconds slipping out
of her high-heeled sandals without Kevin noticing.
She pulled the handle on the door and stepped out
of the car. The second her foot hit the ground, she

took off running in the direction they had come from. Her bare feet slapped lightly on the dirty, warm pavement.

There was a long wire fence along the back of the property, and a field full of bushes beyond it. Simone imagined that, if she could outrun him, she could cut into the field if there was an opening in the fence, or continue on the path until she got to the street. Surely, there would be someone around to help her.

The sound of Kevin swearing loudly rang out in the silence around them; then Simone could hear his feet pounding on the ground as he came after her. She tried to run faster, forgetting to breathe in her efforts. The edge of the building came closer and it appeared that she was holding the distance between them. Adrenaline and desperation pushed her forward, until she stepped on something sharp and jagged with the heel of her left foot.

A large shard of bottle glass had become embedded in her tender heel, but Simone barely felt it at first. Two steps later, her knees buckled and she fell to the ground, scraping her knees raw.

She screamed in frustration and pain, but still managed to stand up again. Simone could only manage to shuffle a few more steps before she could hear his panting breath right behind her. Seconds later, her head exploded with white light and she crumpled to the ground at his feet.

It was almost eight o'clock when Maxwell rang Simone's doorbell. He waited for about a minute, then rang the bell again. Finally, assuming she was in the bathroom or something, he used the spare key she had given him to open the door.

"Simone," he yelled as he walked through the apartment trying to find her. "Simone, where are you?"

Maxwell looked everywhere, including her bedroom closet, then walked back to the living room.

Where could she be? he thought. It was over an hour since she had called him to say she was on her way home.

Trying not to panic, Maxwell called her cell phone for the second time since he got her message. Again, it rang several times before going to voice mail. He hung up, frustrated.

Where the hell is she?

His next logical thought was that she had gone out again after waiting for him to call her back. Maxwell spent another few minutes looking around for a note, or any sign of where she might have gone.

There was nothing.

At some point while searching around, he finally acknowledged the dread that had been burning in the pit of his stomach since the moment he had heard Simone's voice say she had gone to Kevin's apartment. Even though she had sounded fine, and had stated that she was on her way home, everything inside Maxwell screamed that she was in danger. But he had contained his fear, telling himself that he was overreacting.

Now he knew different.

He called Cedric on his cell phone.

"What's up?" his brother asked.

"Are you home yet?" Maxwell asked.

"Yeah, I just stepped in the door."

"Is Simone there?"

"No, I don't think so. Why? Isn't she there?"

"Can you ask Amy if she's spoken to her?"

"Max, what's going on?"

"Ask her, please!" he demanded impatiently.

Cedric finally understood his urgency, and Maxwell could hear him talking to Amy for a few seconds. He also heard Amy say she hadn't spoken to Simone all day.

"Cedric, do you still talk to Donald?"

"Donald? Donald Johnson? It's been a while. Why?"

Maxwell took a deep breath. "Listen, I need you to come and get me again. I'll explain everything to you when you get here."

Thankfully, Cedric heard the seriousness in his brother's voice and arrived back at Simone's place less than fifteen minutes later. Maxwell was waiting for him downstairs.

"Where are we going?" Cedric asked the minute Maxwell slid into the passenger seat.

"I need to find out where Kevin lives. Do you think Donald will tell us?"

"He doesn't have to. They live together in a condo in Midtown. I've been there a couple of times," his brother replied. "Now, do you want to tell me what the hell is going on?"

It took most of the drive for Maxwell to explain everything.

"I told her to stay away from him, but she just wouldn't listen," he told Cedric.

"Maxwell, Kevin's even worse now than he was when we were kids. I've heard some stories over the years that would make your hair stand up. Apparently, he's broke and his dealerships are on the verge of bankruptcy. Donald is still the only one that has any control over him. But if he is taking steroids and catches Simone snooping around, he's likely to do anything."

As he stared out the window at the setting sun,

something clicked in Maxwell's mind. He looked at Cedric, more afraid than he'd ever been in his life.

"Cedric, I think that's exactly what happened to Simone's friend, Natasha. I've been banging my head for days, trying to figure out why Simone was so hell-bent on going through with the search, and it's been right in front of me the whole time. It has nothing to do with the steroids. Simone was trying to find out who had a motive to kill Natasha and make it look like an accident."

The brothers looked at each other, suddenly aware of exactly what they were dealing with.

Chapter 29

Donald Johnson was clearly surprised to see Maxwell and Cedric at his door. He invited them in.

"Wow, Max! I haven't seen you in years man! Last I heard from Cedric, you were living in Canada somewhere," Donald stated.

They stopped in front of the kitchen.

"Yeah," replied Maxwell. "I'm just here for a visit."

"So, how's it going?"

The brothers looked at each other, confirming the need to get right to the point.

"Donald, where is Kevin?" Cedric finally asked.

Donald looked back and forth between them, noticing the look of tension on their faces. "I don't know. Why?"

Maxwell stepped forward to stand directly in front of him, looking Donald hard in the face. "Look, Don. We've all known each other for a long time, right? You and Cedric used to be so close that you were like a brother to me too. Do you know what I'm saying?"

"I know."

"Good. So you know we're not here to pass judgment. We just need to find Kevin. Now!"

"Max, why don't you just tell me what this is all about? I honestly don't know where Kevin is right now."

Maxwell let out a deep breath filled with disappointment. Donald looked like he was telling the truth.

"Was Simone St. Claire here tonight?" Cedric finally asked.

Donald took a step back, then hesitated before answering.

"We know about the steroids, Don," continued Cedric.

"Aw, damn!" muttered Donald.

He turned away from them and folded his arms over his head.

"I tried to get her to leave it alone, Donald, and she didn't tell me she was coming here tonight," Maxwell told him.

Donald finally turned to face them again, dropping his arms to his sides. Everything about his appearance said he felt defeated.

"She was here, but she left a while ago," he told them.

"We know that," said Maxwell. "She left me a message saying she was on her way home. But she never got there, Donald. I know she found the steroids, and you know it too. So I need you to tell us where Kevin is before he does something that we will all regret."

Donald just shook his head.

"I knew this whole title match was a bad idea. Kevin wasn't training right, but he wouldn't listen to me. He kept saying that he would be fine, but I could see he wasn't. That last fight really did some damage, Max," he explained. "Finally, I told him that we should pull out. But Kevin had already started spending the money from the purse and making promises that he couldn't keep. That's when he told me about the supplements."

Maxwell and Cedric looked at each other, now convinced that Simone was in very real danger.

"Where would he have taken her, Donald?" demanded Maxwell.

When Simone slowly came to, it was pitch-black around her. She was lying on a floor that felt like it was carpeted. The musty and stale smell of it made her recoil in disgust. That sudden movement caused her head to pound as though it were cracked open.

Her gasp of pain echoed in the space. She reached up to touch the tender spot behind her right ear, and her fingers came away wet and sticky. She lay back down with her eyes closed, trying to be as still as possible. A wave of nausea washed over her and her mouth filled with bile.

"You're awake."

She risked opening her eyes and found Kevin standing over her. Simone had not heard him come in and wondered if she had passed out again. An open door behind him brought a little light into the room. It appeared to be a small storage area filled with dusty boxes. Out of the corner of her eye, she could make out a discarded boxing glove.

"Where am I?" she whispered. "What have you done to me?"

Kevin ignored her questions. Instead, he bent down and picked her up into his arms as if she were a doll. Simone screamed in agony as her head bobbed up and down. He continued forward, completely unaffected by her suffering. She started sobbing quietly, finally giving in to the helplessness of her situation.

When he stopped, they were in a large open space that was empty except for a few pieces of workout equipment. Simone watched in horror as Kevin put her down on top of a filthy old piece of carpet spread out on the floor.

"No! No, Kevin. You don't want to do this."

"Shut up," he commanded dispassionately.

"People will be looking for me. They know that I was with you tonight. You're not going to get away with this, Kevin."

"That's right. You were with me, and then you left, remember? Donald saw you leave and so did my doorman," he explained simply. "What happened to you after has nothing to do with me."

He straddled her waist between his knees, trapping her arms against her sides. Simone tried to hold back a sob, but it broke through her lips with raw desperation. "How can you do this?"

"You brought this on yourself! I treated you good, but you didn't appreciate it. Then you try to take my career and my reputation away from me? You deserve whatever you get."

Kevin brushed his hands down the sides of her face until they settled around her slender neck.

"No, it wasn't like that. I swear!" she exclaimed, twisting her head back and forth, trying to elude his grasp.

"Shhhh. It's over now."

Simone's eyes widened at the madness that shone in his. She tried desperately to break free as his fingers tightened around her windpipe.

"Kevin!"

His name was shouted from somewhere behind them, but Kevin didn't seem to hear it. His fingers continued to squeeze her neck, his eyes closed as though to block out the terror in hers.

"Kevin, let her go!"

Donald ran across the room and threw himself forward, using his body to knock his brother off Simone. Kevin fell to the side, finally releasing his stranglehold on her neck. She immediately rolled away from him onto her side, struggling to suck in air through her bruised windpipe.

Kevin recovered quickly and reached for her again, trying to finish what he had started. Donald pushed him over, pinning Kevin with his weight.

"Kevin, it's over. It's all over, man."

"I should have listened to you, Don. This is all my fault. You told me to get rid of her, but I didn't listen."

"No, not like this. I can't let you do this."

Simone rolled farther away from them, coming to rest on her stomach while still wheezing and sucking in air. The pain in her head made her want to throw up. She swallowed hard.

Suddenly, large hands fell on her waist, turning her over.

"Oh God, Simone," muttered Maxwell. "What has he done to you?"

Blinded by pain and fear, she struggled violently against the touch, convinced it was Kevin again.

"No, please!"

"Simone, it me. It's Maxwell. Simone!"

She went limp in his arms.

Maxwell froze, staring down at her face, deathly still and smeared with blood and dirt.

"Oh, baby!" he muttered, running his hand gently along her neck, desperately searching for a pulse.

"Is she okay?" asked Cedric as he approached them.

"I don't know! I think I feel a pulse, but I don't know! Look what's he's done to her!"

Cedric looked over at Donald and Kevin just a few feet away. Donald was still on top of his brother, trying to calm him down, but Kevin was struggling wildly, babbling incoherently.

"We have to get out of here, Maxwell. Now!" Cedric whispered urgently.

"No one is going anywhere," stated Kevin.

He had managed to throw Donald off him and now lay on his back with his gun pointed at them. Cedric and Maxwell froze.

Kevin swiftly stood up and walked over to the three of them huddled on the floor. He then blinked a few times, recognizing his old friends for the first time, but not understanding why they were there. Then he started laughing. It caused a chill to go up Maxwell's spine. He tightened his grip on Simone.

"Cedric, is that you? Max? Damn! What're you guys doing here?" he asked with a silly grin on his face and the gun still pointed at them. "Donald, look who's here."

Donald used that moment to rush at his brother, knocking them both onto the floor in a tangle of arms and legs. They rolled around, back and forth, as they fought for control of the weapon.

Maxwell swept Simone up into his arms and started running for the door with Cedric right on his heels. The gunshot went off just before they reached the exit, echoing riotously in the large space.

Chapter 30

The story was all over the news by Monday morning. Two days later, Scott Claus published his report on the downward spiral of boxing superstar Kevin Johnson. It detailed past injuries, illegal steroid use, and deep financial trouble. The media ate it up.

Maxwell was still in Atlanta as it all unfolded.

After Kevin's gun went off during the struggle with Donald, Maxwell continued running from the abandoned boxing gym with Simone held tightly in his arms. When he reached Cedric's car, he opened the back door and gently laid her across the seat. Her body remained limp and her face looked ashen and lifeless. Cedric arrived a few seconds later.

"I think he's dead!" Cedric exclaimed. "Donald shot him, Max, and I think Kevin is dead."

"Oh God!" moaned Maxwell.

The brothers took a few seconds to come to terms with the disastrous outcome of the last few hours.

"He's just sitting there now, holding Kevin's head in his lap and crying," Cedric added. "We have to call the police."

Maxwell nodded, lowering his head as Donald's loss hit him in the pit of his chest. God forbid it could be Cedric or Simone lying there shot dead on that dusty floor. The thought was enough to make him sick with fear and he could only pray that Simone was going to be okay.

The ambulance and police arrived a few minutes later. Cedric stayed behind at the scene while Maxwell rode with Simone to the hospital. During the drive, Simone had woken up, but was clearly in a lot of pain. She recognized Maxwell and even managed to squeeze his hand. The simple movement made him bow his head as tears of relief ran down his face.

The doctors kept Simone in the emergency room until early Monday morning. They explained to Maxwell that most of her injuries were superficial, but the bleeding from her scalp and her unconsciousness were from a vicious gun butt to the back of her head. After cleaning her wounds and adding a few stitches, they let her go home with strict instructions to rest for several days.

Maxwell called his work and let them know he would need another week off to deal with a personal emergency. He then canceled his return ticket to Toronto, uncertain of when he would be ready to leave Simone alone. It was several more days before he felt comfortable enough to reschedule his flight for the coming Sunday.

Simone was feeling much better by the end of the week. Her head wound was healing nicely, as were her other cuts, though she still limped from the gash in her heel. Still, Maxwell had balked at her suggestion that they have a few people over for lunch on Saturday afternoon, including her parents, who had flown home from Connecticut several days earlier. But she had insisted, telling him that she wanted her family and friends to meet him before he returned home.

Augustine and Annabelle St. Claire now sat with Simone in the living room, along with Amy, Cedric, and Maya. Maxwell was in the kitchen, putting together a round of drinks for everyone.

"Here, son, let me help you with that," offered Simone's father as he walked into the room.

"Thank you, sir," Maxwell replied as he handed over two of the beers he struggled with.

"Augustine, please."

Maxwell nodded, glancing at the older gentleman. He was exactly as Maxwell had pictured him from all that Simone talked about: tall and lanky, and with a quiet voice. His wife, Annabelle, was as beautiful as her daughter, and the picture of refined grace.

He had met Simone's parents briefly the day after Kevin was shot when they had flown home early from their summer in Connecticut. Though they were clearly shocked and worried about their daughter, they were both kind to him, and thanked him for being there to save their daughter. Today was the first time that he was able to spend some quality time with them, and he felt it was going well so far.

"Simone has told us a lot about you in the last few weeks. I'm glad that we finally got to meet you," Augustine continued. "But I must admit, I'm a little concerned about the fact that you are living out of the country."

It took Maxwell a couple of moments to realize that her father was essentially asking about his intentions with Simone. He wanted to smile at the old-fashioned notion, but remembered that here in the South, men took that sort of thing very seriously.

"I understand that, sir. Simone and I have talked about it quite a bit. I haven't told Simone yet, but I've done some interviewing with a couple of engineering firms here in Atlanta. If everything goes well, I hope to move back here by early fall."

"That's good to know. And what does that mean for you and my daughter?"

This time, Maxwell did smile at Augustine's persistence. "I am in love with your daughter, sir. My intention is to ask her to marry me, and I pray that she accepts my proposal."

The two men looked at each other, assessing the situation and coming to terms with the commitment that Maxwell was making.

Finally, Augustine nodded and reached out to put an arm around Maxwell's shoulder. "Good, son. That's good to hear. If you need any help convincing her, let me know."

Maxwell broke out laughing and the two men walked back to join the small group. They handed out the drinks, and then Maxwell sat beside Simone, taking her hand in his.

"Is everything okay?" she asked. "My dad wasn't giving you a hard time, was he?"

Maxwell kissed the back of his hand, then smiled into her eyes.

"Not at all," he replied easily.

"Good, 'cause my mom's in love with you now and I think she's petrified that he will do something to send you running."

Maxwell flashed her one of his big smiles. "Well, your mom will be happy to know that the next time I return to Atlanta, I'm here to stay."

The mocking smile on her lips faltered as Simone sensed the seriousness in his words.

"What do you mean?" she finally asked.

"I mean that I've decided to move back here, permanently."

"Maxwell!" she gasped, throwing herself into his arms despite the surprised looks from the people around them.

"I almost lost you, Simone, and that scared the hell out of me. You are my heart and soul, and I want to be right here with you for the rest of my life."

She pulled back from their embrace to look deep into his eyes while hers pooled with tears of joy.

"How do you feel about a fall wedding in Jamaica?" he added finally.

"I think I know a good resort," Simone replied before he pulled her into his arms again.